LOVING ENEMY

ST. Den.

LOVING ENEMY

Catherine Cross

CHIVERS
THORNDIKE

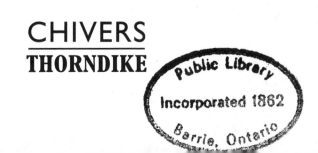

This Large Print edition is published by BBC Audiobooks Ltd, Bath, England and by Thorndike Press®, Waterville, Maine, USA.

Published in 2004 in the U.K. by arrangement with the author.

Published in 2004 in the U.S. by arrangement with Mary Cross.

U.K. Hardcover   ISBN 0–7540–7799–3 (Chivers Large Print)
U.K. Softcover   ISBN 0–7540–9977–6 (Camden Large Print)
U.S. Softcover   ISBN 0–7862–6310–5 (Nightingale)

The text of this Large Print edition is unabridged.
Other aspects of the book may vary from the original edition.

Set in 16 pt. New Times Roman.

Printed in Great Britain on acid-free paper.

British Library Cataloguing in Publication Data available

Library of Congress Control Number: 2003116428

CHAPTER ONE

Kate hung on grimly to the overhead strap, keeping her balance with difficulty in the swaying airport bus. Torrential rain drummed on the roof, almost drowning out the sound of the engine and water trickled off her chestnut brown hair, running down the back of her neck.

She shivered. If this is May, she thought, someone ought to remind the weather!

On the floor at her feet lay a rather disreputable package. The very thought of what was in the parcel made her shudder, and she knew with certainty that she could not possibly take it with her on the aircraft.

She wondered, not for the first time that day, why she had allowed Aunt Nell to talk her into trying. She smiled wryly to herself, remembering the conversation at breakfast.

'Now, Kate, dear, it won't be too difficult. It's well-wrapped, you needn't even think about what's in it, if you don't want to.'

'But Aunt Nell—'

'No! No buts, my dear! Just remember, you're doing it for your father.'

Aunt Nell thought that people were capable of far more than they believed possible, so eventually, not really to Kate's surprise, Nell persuaded her to take the parcel with her when she left for the airport.

Next to the parcel lay an overnight bag, heavy now with the additional weight of two bottles of Australian Chardonnay wine.

This had been a good business trip for her. Meetings with two wine shippers in London had resulted, after tasting, with Kate deciding to include half a dozen new wines in her own shop. Stocks for the shop were being despatched in a few days, but the two bottles were a present for her parents.

Francine and David Hamilton had been delighted when she had said she wanted to start her own business, and had done everything they could to help her make a success of it.

Kate loved her parents and would do anything for them. Well, almost. She looked down at the parcel at her feet and sighed.

When Kate left her aunt's flat for Heathrow just after lunch, rain was falling from leaden skies. Finding a taxi had proved unusually difficult, and by the time Kate managed to find one, both she and the parcel were soaked.

If she was going to get rid of it she knew it would have to be soon, before the bus reached the aircraft. She glanced around to see if anyone was watching her, but, thankfully, her fellow passengers all seemed preoccupied.

Two young children bounced noisily up and down on their seats while their parents smiled indulgently, making no effort to quieten them.

Farther down the bus an old lady, sitting on her own, rubbed a gloved hand over a small area of steamed-up window, and peered out.

It was now or never.

Kate nudged the soggy paper parcel with her foot. Nothing happened. A knot in the string had snagged on a metal grip-bar on the floor and the parcel refused to budge. She pushed harder and it slowly disappeared under the seat.

How she was going to explain the absence of the parcel to her mother and Aunt Nell she didn't know, but at least she wouldn't have to see it again. Closing warm, brown eyes she breathed a sigh of relief.

When she opened them she was startled to find a pair of navy blue eyes staring straight back at her. They belonged to a tanned, masculine face. Not good-looking in the strictest sense of the word, but arresting.

Kate thought that you could tell a person's character by their eyes, and his looked as if he had seen a great deal of life and still found it interesting, even amusing. He had a wide mouth, the top lip slightly thinner than the bottom, indicating, to Kate's mind, a sensual nature. His thick, dark hair was brushed straight back from his face.

As she watched, the corners of his mouth curved upwards in a smile and one eye slowly winked at her.

She felt the heat run up her neck and over

3

her heart-shaped face and she looked away quickly. It amazed Kate to think that, even now, at the age of twenty six, she could still blush like a teenager. Nibbling on her bottom lip, she wondered if he had seen her trying to hide the parcel. She hoped not. The thought of someone telling her she had left it behind, or, even worse, running after her and giving it back was unbearable.

The airport bus swerved to a halt at the side of a small plane and the other passengers began to gather up their belongings. Kate bent down to pick up her overnight bag. To her alarm she saw that the parcel had finally disintegrated. The large, yellow beak and white-feathered neck of a plump goose lolled in the aisle of the bus, one glassy eye staring up at her reproachfully. She shrank back in horror and swallowed a startled cry.

All rational thought gone, she pushed past passengers in a desperate effort to get away and hurried up the steps to the plane, expecting any minute to be called back for her abandoned parcel.

On board, refusing the air hostess's help, she found her row number without trouble, put her overnight bag in the overhead locker and settled her slim figure thankfully into her seat next to a window. The bustle of people stowing their hand luggage and getting settled in their seats carried on around her unnoticed as she breathed deeply and tried to blank

4

the last few minutes from her mind. Kate reckoned that when the plane had taken off it would be too late for anyone to discover who had left the parcel on the bus, and she would be safe.

She slowly became aware of an insistent voice at her side.

'My seat, I believe?'

'Pardon?' Startled, she half turned in her seat and found herself gazing into the face that had winked at her on the bus. He looked pointedly at the seat next to her and then back.

'Oh—yes. Sorry,' she said, removing her handbag and pushing it under her seat.

He sat down. Seen close to, he was older than she first thought, probably in his early thirties. Laughter lines crinkled at the outer edges of his eyes and mouth. He was tall, well over six foot she guessed, her eyes taking in the expensive, tan, leather jacket, spotted now with rain, and the well-cut black cords as they hugged his thighs.

'Your first trip to Cornwall?' he asked, running his hand through his thick, dark hair in an effort to control an unruly lock.

Kate's mind had already returned to the problem of the parcel and she dragged her thoughts together in an effort to concentrate on what he was saying. She forced a tight smile.

'No, I live there. I've been to London on business.'

He was about to say something else when an air hostess, speaking through a microphone, said, 'Ladies and gentlemen, may I have your attention please. Before I go through the Emergency Procedure I have a parcel here which someone has inadvertently left on the bus. We have repacked it and would like to give it back to its owner.'

She held up the parcel and waited. No-one spoke. People twisted in their seats to look around at their fellow passengers expectantly. Kate hurriedly pulled out the Emergency Procedure leaflet from the back pocket of the seat in front of her and pretended to study it.

The air hostess spoke again. 'Now, ladies and gentlemen, I am sure I'm not giving away any secrets when I say that the parcel contains a rather lovely goose, and unless someone claims it soon I shall be taking it home for my week-end lunch.' Passengers started to laugh.

Next to Kate her companion put up his hand and said in a loud voice, 'It's mine.'

A few passengers glanced his way, shouted, 'Hooray' and clapped their hands.

Kate gasped. The man had a nerve! Who did he think he was, claiming a parcel he had no right to? She immediately wanted to stand up and shout out that it was her parcel, but even as the thought entered her head she knew it was impossible now. After all, she had left it on the bus deliberately, and she didn't really want it back, did she? She shuddered. The

6

answer to that question was a definite 'no'.

Brown eyes ventured a sideways peep at blue. He was looking at her, his eyes questioning. She refused to respond and, giving him a withering look, turned away and hunched farther over her leaflet, pretending to read.

He leaned towards her, gently took the leaflet out of her hands, turned it up the right way, and gave it back, smiling.

Kate fumed. Not only was this man stealing her parcel, he was making her look like an idiot into the bargain, and he had the audacity to smile while he was doing it! Not that there was much she could do about it.

She stuffed the leaflet mutinously back into the seat pocket and, turning away from him, looked out of the window.

The air hostess, smart in her uniform of yellow and white striped shirt and navy skirt, brought the parcel down the aisle.

'Sorry to have troubled you,' the man said. 'I forgot I left it on the bus.'

'No trouble, sir,' the girl replied, giving him what Kate thought, half-turning and viewing the scene from under her mascara-tipped eyelashes, was a far too friendly smile. 'All part of the service. Luckily the parcel had broken open on the bus and we could see what it contained, or we may well have had a bomb scare on our hands. We have to be careful about security even on a domestic flight like this. No harm done, though. I'll put this in the locker, shall I?'

After stowing the parcel away she smiled again, and with a, 'I hope you have a good flight,' moved forward to the front of the plane to begin the Emergency Procedure routine.

He turned towards Kate, his expression giving nothing away. 'I've heard of cooking your goose, but abandoning it on an airport bus is quite novel!' His mouth quirked up at the corners, became a grin and Kate, against her will, found herself smiling with him. The parcel was proving more difficult to lose than she had anticipated.

Embarrassed, she realised she would have to give him some sort of explanation. 'I suppose I'd better come clean,' she volunteered.

'Definitely. I'm intrigued—but not before we've introduced ourselves. I'm Daniel Ashcroft.' He took her right hand in his and squeezed gently.

Kate felt a tingle of excitement run to her fingertips. 'Katherine Hamilton,' she said. 'Most people call me Kate.'

Just then the plane gave a jolt and began to move forward. It taxied out to the runway and joined the queue of aircraft ready for take-off.

Kate started to explain. 'Well— It's my father's birthday on Sunday. We're giving a surprise lunch party for him. Goose is Pa's favourite, but we don't keep any of our own.

8

So Aunt Nell decided to get one from her game dealer as her present for him. Anyway, I was very conveniently in London for a few days and Aunt Nell expected me to bring it home, and it took me a while to find a taxi.'

'So you and the goose got wet, and that's why it needed repacking?'

'Yes. When the parcel fell to pieces on the bus I couldn't bear to pick it up. But how on earth did you know it was mine?'

'You've got an expressive face, Kate. I could see you had a problem on the bus, although I couldn't tell what it was. What finally convinced me was the upside-down leaflet.'

'I could just have been afraid of flying!' she said, indignantly.

He laughed. 'Running up the steps to get on the plane hardly seems to be the action of someone afraid of flying.'

'But why bail me out?' Kate enquired.

'Who could resist such beautiful, brown eyes? Seriously though, why didn't you claim it yourself?'

Kate crossed one slim ankle over the other and played with the gold bracelet on her wrist. Looking out of the window she saw small houses and roads far below and was surprised to find that she had missed the take-off completely. She turned back to Daniel with a rueful expression on her face.

'When I was five, my brother Jeff gave me a "present" of a dead rabbit, which frightened

9

me half to death. He didn't mean to scare me, but since then I've never been able to get near a dead animal without a feeling of revulsion. I made a real effort with the goose, but in the end it didn't work out. I'm only surprised I managed to get it as far as the bus. Thanks to you, Pa's going to be very happy.'

He smiled.

'The least I can do is ask you to the party.'

Kate almost gasped aloud, surprised that her normal reticence had been completely knocked out by the good-looking man sitting next to her. Whatever made me say that? We've only just met, for heaven's sake, hardly the time to be issuing invitations. He's probably even now thinking of a polite excuse. Serves me right if he was, she thought, wishing wholeheartedly that she could have grabbed the words back before they reached him.

She had to admit, though, that few people would have been so quick to sum up the situation and help her out, as he had done. Surely that deserved a reward, didn't it?

The impromptu invitation couldn't have been because you find him so attractive, could it, a little voice piped up in her head. She fought the suggestion down and ignored it.

Well . . . nothing ventured, nothing gained, as Aunt Nell was fond of saying.

'My father owns Home Farm Stud just outside Truro. He breeds horses. It's easy to find if you don't know the area.'

10

He gazed at her for what seemed like an eternity, searching her face, and rewarded her with a smile that would melt a polar ice-cap. She felt her bones turn to jelly, and was glad she was sitting down.

'I'd love to come, Kate. Thanks.'

They butterflied from one topic of conversation to another and she discovered they had a great deal in common, including the same quirky sense of humour. The rest of the journey passed in a haze for Kate, and it was over all too soon.

On their arrival at Newquay Airport she felt brave enough to manage the parcel herself as it was now rewrapped. They said goodbye, Daniel to locate his hire car, and Kate to find her brother, who was collecting her.

The verbal sparring with Daniel had heightened her colour, making her sparkle with vitality, and her steps had a spring to them as she moved on graceful legs to where she saw her brother waiting.

'Hello, Pudding, had a good trip?' Jeff asked, giving her a quick peck on the cheek.

'Mmm . . . wonderful.'

He took her overnight bag and the parcel, stowing them in the boot of his car.

'So, what's new?' Kate asked, as he started the engine, put the car in gear and headed it towards the airport exit. 'Has Pa had any news about Polventon Manor since I've been away?'

'Yes. Bad, though. He heard yesterday.

The council has definitely granted planning permission, so it looks as if Jack Trevelyan will go ahead and buy the place now.'

'Oh, Jeff! How terrible! Isn't there anything Pa can do to stop him?'

'Not really, Pud. Apparently Trevelyan put a large deposit on the Manor before he applied for planning permission, so the sale is really only a formality.'

'But there must be something we can do, surely? Colonel Jeffreys was such a sweet old boy. He would never have wanted to see Pa in this sort of trouble. Oh, why did he have to die?'

Jeff laughed. 'He was eighty-seven, Kate. Anyway, Pa should have bought the forty acres years ago instead of renting it. That way, when the colonel died it wouldn't have made any difference who bought the Manor.'

Polventon Manor's land ran alongside her father's, and, until the colonel's death at the end of last year, he had the use of it for grazing his brood mares and their foals. A new owner meant that her father would lose the grazing rights.

Her father's stud had originally been the estate farm of Polventon Manor before Colonel Jeffreys sold it to him.

Kate looked at her brother. 'Why would Pa have needed to buy the land? They were such good friends.'

'That was the problem, I think. Pa didn't

want to upset him by asking. The colonel wanted a steady income and preferred Pa to rent the grazing. He did tell me once that as he'd already sold us the home farm he didn't feel he ought to sell off any more of the estate, as big houses without land weren't worth much.'

Kate sighed. 'What is worth anything, these days?' She thought for a while and then, frowning, said, 'Any idea why Pa dislikes Jack Trevelyan so much?'

Jeff shook his head. 'Not a clue. I heard Aunt Nell say once that they used to be close friends when they were young.' He shrugged his shoulders. 'Who knows?'

Kate laid a hand on her brother's arm. 'Can't you give him some of your land, Jeff, or at least lend it to him for a while until he gets something more permanent sorted out?'

Her brother had a small farm on the other side of the village from their parents, and Kate, not knowing much about farming, though it might be possible for her father to use some of Jeff's land temporarily.

He took a hand off the steering wheel for a second and gave Kate's hand a reassuring squeeze, his grey eyes clouded with disappointment.

'I tried that, but he refused. You know how independent he is.'

'If you ask me, he's just plain stubborn!'

Jeff glanced at her and tried not to laugh.

13

'Listen to the pot calling the kettle black,' he said. 'Besides, although the farm is paying its way right now, losing the use of forty acres would put a different light on things. Pa knows that, that's why he's refusing my help.

'Anyway, let's change the subject. You'll hear about this again tonight, no doubt. Don't forget, Mum's expecting you for supper. Talking of food, have you got the goose?'

'Yes.'

'So, Nell persuaded you to bring it, then?'

'Sort of.' Kate wasn't about to tell her brother what had happened on the plane. If he knew, he would never stop teasing her about it.

'I'm amazed!'

'I had some help,' she said, trying to look innocent.

He shot her a shrewd look from under thick, dark eyebrows.

'What sort of help?'

'Never you mind.' Kate smiled smugly. 'Just get on with the chauffeuring.'

Jeff threaded the car through the early evening traffic. 'Secrets, huh? Well, if I'm just the chauffeur you'd better tell me where you want dropping off.'

When Jeff drew the blue sports car to a halt outside the back entrance to Kate's wine shop the evening rush was almost over. He took her overnight bag from the boot. 'I'll drop the goose off at Mum's on my way home.'

'OK. Tell her I'll be over by eight. See you

then, and thanks for the lift,' she said, angling her cheek upwards to receive his kiss. She waved as he roared off down the road.

The shop was closed, and Sally, Kate's best friend who worked in the wine shop, had gone home. On the desk in her tiny office Kate found notes which Sally had left for her, bringing her up to date with what had been happening in the shop while she had been in London. She read the notes, then walked around the shop, letting the familiar smells wash over her. She sighed contentedly. It was good to be home.

Her love of wine came directly from her French mother and her father, who had brought their children up from an early age in the true French tradition, by mixing a little wine with their water at meals. As Kate grew up she began to appreciate the subtle differences in aromas and flavours, and by the time she was fifteen she could easily tell which country and area a wine came from purely by the colour, aroma and taste of the wine.

Neither parent was surprised when she chose a career in the wine trade and both had been very supportive. They had encouraged her when she left college and moved to Bristol to work for a large wine shipper, where she spent three years gaining experience in the trade and taking exams.

On her twenty-first birthday her parents had bought her the property which now housed her wine business. That had been five years ago, and not once had she regretted her decision to come home to Cornwall.

The shop was situated in a small, cobbled street near the cathedral. The ground floor was taken over with the shop itself, her office and the wine stores. Upstairs there had been more storage space, so she had a tiny bathroom and kitchen installed, and turned it into a small, but comfortable, home for herself.

After carefully setting the burglar alarm and locking up, Kate made her way up the wrought-iron steps in the yard which led to her flat.

Terracotta pots lined the edges of the steps and brightly-coloured geraniums were flowering in them, promising a riot of colour when they spilled over their pots in the coming summer months. White walls reflected the last of the day's sun and rain-soaked London seemed like another world away.

As she showered and dressed, Kate thought over what her brother had told her on the journey back from the airport. Breeding horses had always been her father's passion and Kate knew he would be devastated if he had to curtail his breeding programme.

Pulling a soft, raspberry-coloured sweater on over her white, cotton trousers and, finally, clipping on large, gilt ear-rings, she collected the two bottles of white wine she had put

16

aside. She made her way down the steps into the yard to her car and set off on the ten-minute drive to her parents' house.

*   *   *

Kate's tyres scrunched on gravel as she parked her car at the back of the farmhouse. It was long and low, with thick, stone walls that had weathered the gales of centuries. Roses clambered over the south-facing wall, buds already opening on the stems.

In the distance across the field she could just make out the Tresillian River and the trees on the opposite bank, although dusk was falling fast now. Lights blazed in the house and as Kate walked towards the door she could see, through the lattice windows, her mother busy in the kitchen.

'*Chérie!* How wonderful! You're home!'

Kate put down the bottles of wine she had been carrying and the two women hugged and kissed each other. Her mother, grey hair smartly cut and classical clothes worn with flair, was the epitome of a chic Frenchwoman, despite living in England for over thirty years. Violet eyes sparkled at her daughter from an immaculately made-up face, still beautiful in maturity.

'Well, my darling, tell me all about the trip. Did you have a good time? Find any nice wines? Meet any interesting people?'

Kate smiled at her mother's exuberance.

'Steady on, Mum. One question at a time! There's a new Australian Chardonnay that I'm about to stock. I've brought back a couple of bottles for you and Pa to try. If I put them in ice and water now we can have a glass before dinner. Where's Pa?'

'Upstairs having the shower. He'll be down soon.'

Kate half-filled an ice bucket with cold water and rummaged around in the freezer for a tray of ice-cubes.

'While he's out of hearing, do you need any help for Sunday?'

'No, darling, thank you. Everything is organised, and it is still a secret. I think he knows nothing. Nell will be down on Saturday so I shall have plenty of help. Just make sure that you and Jeff keep him busy on Sunday morning. Take him riding, or something.

'Jeff tells me he has asked Sally to come. I don't suppose you have invited anyone, *chérie*?' The words seemed innocent enough, and Kate couldn't help rising to the bait.

'Well, I have, as a matter of fact.'

Her mother smiled to herself. 'Oh, that's nice, darling. Do we know him?'

'Now, why do you always suppose it's a man? I could be bringing a woman friend.'

A sigh emanated from her mother's side of the kitchen. 'Oh, well . . . is it someone we know?'

18

'No, I've only just met him myself, so you'll have to save your questions for another time.' Kate could tell her mother was bursting with curiosity and trying hard not to ask any questions. She laughed.

'Ah, you like him!' her mother cried, delightedly.

'Well of course I like him. I'm hardly going to invite someone I can't stand the sight of, now, am I?'

Kate started cutting a French loaf for the bread basket, and noticed a bottle of red burgundy on the kitchen counter. The cork had been drawn, allowing the wine to breathe. She eyed the label suspiciously.

'Hmm . . . Gevry Chambertin. If I hadn't already heard the bad news about Polventon from Jeff, this bottle would have given the game away. You're the only person I know who opens a bottle of really good wine whenever disaster strikes. Most people keep the good stuff for celebrations.'

Francine Hamilton smiled at her daughter. 'Worse than that! A half bottle has also gone into the Coq au Vin. But don't tell your papa!'

Kate laughed. 'Your secret's safe with me.'

Her mother gave a small Gallic shrug. 'Anyway, what is the point of keeping the good wine for when you're feeling good? Keep the best for when you need cheering up, I say. The good times take care of themselves.'

She bent to take a casserole dish out of the

19

Aga, lifted the lid, and peered into its depths. A mouthwatering smell of chicken, wine and herbs wafted around the kitchen. '*Bon.* It is ready. We only await the men.'

Later, as they ate dinner, the talk inevitably turned to Jack Trevelyan and Polventon Manor.

'Now I won't have the use of the colonel's land next door there's nothing for it but to cut my breeding programme,' her father said. 'I can't see any other way around it.'

'It is so annoying,' Francine said, leaning across the table and squeezing her husband's hand in sympathy, 'especially now that you are beginning to get a reputation as a good breeder of three-day event horses, non? This is not done easily.'

David Hamilton bred Arab-Hanovarian crosses and only last year Claire Bridgeman, the country's top three-day eventer, had bought a gelding from him, and was already winning competitions with the horse.

'If only the lease on the land didn't expire next month,' he said. 'It doesn't give me much time to find more grazing. Besides, I didn't expect there to be any difficulty in buying it.'

'Then,' Kate said, helping herself to cheese from the board, 'I don't see any way around it. You'll just have to ask Jack Trevelyan to sell the land to you.'

Her father's face turned red with anger. 'I'm not asking that ruddy man for any favours, nor

20

are any of my family. Is that understood?' he thundered at them. 'It's bad enough that he is buying the Manor, and not someone else. We are not going cap in hand to him for the land. I refuse to let any one of you have anything to do with that family.'

'Kate, you are very naughty! You shouldn't tease your papa, you know his blood pressure won't stand it.'

Kate, immediately contrite, apologised. 'But why does he need all that land? I thought he wanted to turn the Manor into an upmarket hotel? Surely a few acres is all he needs?'

'The land at the back has direct access to the foreshore,' her father said. 'They won't want their guests walking through a field of horses to get to the jetty and the water. Besides, how many would remember to close the gates? We've got valuable stock in those fields, not all of it ours.'

'What I don't understand,' Jeff said, 'is why he needs another hotel. Isn't one enough? At his age most people are winding down, not expanding.'

Francine added to the conversation. 'Lily, his wife, has not been keeping well lately. I've heard he's asked her son to come home to set up this new place in partnership with him, and run it. That way his mother will see more of him.'

Kate, curious, asked, 'Do you know any more, Mum?'

'Only that he is the "bees knees" as far as Lily is concerned. And that's just as it should be.' She nodded her head emphatically. 'At least he is qualified for the job, apparently. He's been doing hotel management in Europe for a few years. Austria, Switzerland, France . . . so I hear. According to rumour, he's due here soon from Australia where he's been visiting vineyards and such.'

'And do we know who this paragon is?' Jeff asked.

'Mmm? Oh, yes,' his mother said. 'He's called Daniel Ashcroft.'

CHAPTER TWO

Kate's hand moved involuntarily and knocked over her almost full glass of red wine. It rolled along the top of the polished oak table, spilling its contents in all directions as it rolled.

Everyone jumped to their feet except Kate, who sat in a state of shock, only vaguely aware of what was happening around her. There has to be a mistake, she thought. There must be two Daniel Ashcrofts. But even as the thought flashed into her mind, she knew, with a sinking heart, that the man she had met on the plane and the one her family were discussing now had to be one and the same.

Jeff ran to fetch the roll of kitchen paper

which hung in its rack on the wall.

'What ever made you do that?' he asked in a exasperated tone. 'Clumsy idiot.'

Her parents mopped at the wine on the table with their napkins. 'Don't be silly, Jeff, she didn't do it on purpose,' her mother said.

Kate sat and watched the red wine dripping from the table on to her lap. It had already soaked through the napkin and into her trousers. She started to dab ineffectually at the stains with the soiled napkin.

Francine gave her a sharp look. 'Here, let me do that,' she said, taking the cloth away from Kate. She fetched an opened bottle of the white wine they had been trying before dinner and poured some over the red wine stains on Kate's trousers.

'Now, *chérie,* you must get out of these so that I can deal with them. If we are lucky there will be no trace of red left, but hurry. Go and find a skirt of mine you can get into and bring these back immediately. *Vite! Vite!* She clapped her hands to indicate the urgency of the situation.

Upstairs, flicking hangers along the rail in her mother's wardrobe, Kate tried to pull herself together. She thought back to her conversation with Daniel on the aircraft. They had been so busy discussing things of mutual interest, there hadn't been time to talk about their own work.

Had he known who I was? Could he even

have planned it that way? No, don't be silly, she argued with herself, we had only just met. He couldn't have known who I was.

On the other hand, he did take quite a while to make up his mind to say yes to the invitation, she remembered pulling on a skirt.

If he has only just come back to this country perhaps his step-father hasn't had time to mention us yet. Well, one thing was for sure, he mustn't come on Sunday. She tried to imagine what her father would say. After tonight's little outburst she dreaded to think.

Later, in bed in one of her parents' guest rooms where she always slept when she stayed for supper, Kate tossed and turned. The duvet tangled round her feet and legs as she tried desperately to find a solution. When sleep finally caught up with her just before dawn, her problem was still not resolved.

*   *   *

The next morning, just after nine, the door to the wine shop burst open and Sally walked in, a vision in a red and black suit, her dark brown curls bobbing happily on her head, a cheeky grin in place.

'Hi. Sorry I'm a bit late this morning. Sam was playing up again, so I had to take him across to Mum's still in his pyjamas, the little devil.'

Kate smiled. Sally's four-year-old son was a

darling, and the image of his father who had died so tragically in an accident three years ago, but a bit of a handful nonetheless, and spoiled rotten by his grandmother.

Kate privately thought that it would be a good thing when Jeff married Sally. They had been going out together for a couple of years, and Jeff and Sam were devoted to each other. A good dose of stability was probably what the youngster needed most. Kate also thought how wonderful it would be to have Sally as a sister-in-law.

'Anyway, how was London?' Sally asked, dragging off her jacket and tucking her handbag under the long wooden counter. She eyed her friend quizzically. 'No, on second thoughts, don't answer that. You look appalling!'

'Thanks a lot,' Kate said, half-heartedly checking the bottles on the tasting table to see if any needed replacing.

'What you need is a cup of coffee. I'll go and make one.'

Sally returned a few minutes later with the coffee and two bars of chocolate.

'Here,' she said, handing one to Kate, 'get that inside you and you'll feel a lot better.'

Kate wasn't sure she could agree, but, to please her friend, unwrapped one end of it and took a bite. She was surprised to find that the caramel and chocolate improved her spirits with every mouthful.

25

'Right, now when you're ready, let's get down to the problem,' Sally said, 'because no matter what you say, you've obviously got one.'

'Is it so obvious?'

'To me it is. I've known you too long. There isn't much I don't know about you, or you about me, come to that. So what's bothering you? Is it the business?'

Kate shook her head, her mouth full of chocolate.

'That's good. Then it can only be a man. There are only two things I've ever known you to lose sleep over and men are one of them,' Sally declared, having another sip of coffee.

'I know you're not the sort of person to wear your heart on your sleeve, Kate, but it might help to talk about it. Two heads, and all that.'

In the course of the morning during gaps when they weren't filling shelves, taking telephone orders and helping customers choose their wines, Kate told Sally the whole story.

'Mmm . . . that's a tricky one,' Sally said when Kate had finished. 'What do you think you'll do?'

Kate shrugged her shoulders. 'There isn't much I can do except try and put him off.'

'What a waste,' Sally said, making Kate laugh.

In the afternoon, during a quiet moment, Kate tried to contact Daniel at his step-father's

26

hotel. She considered the withdrawal of an invitation to be extremely bad manners, but didn't know what else to do. So it was with a heavy heart that she found the hotel's phone number and dialled. She had to keep Daniel away from her father, even it it meant that she would probably never see him again.

What sort of person would want anything to do with someone who issued an invitation and then backed out of it? Her shoulders slumped at the thought.

She was so sure that she would be able to speak to him it didn't occur to her that he might not be there, but each time she phoned she was politely informed that Mr Ashcroft was not in. Eventually she had to admit defeat. All she could do now was to head him off at the party, if he turned up.

*   *   *

The Sunday morning sun shone in a cloudless sky, but Kate, pulling on her jodhpurs and riding boots, was depressed. She had the feeling that today was going to be a disaster. Rather like watching a runaway truck speeding away downhill, she could visualise the crash when it reached the bottom, but was powerless to do anything to stop it.

Picking up her riding hat and gloves, together with a small overnight bag containing the clothes she would be wearing to the party, the drove over to her parents' house.

As she drove along the approach to the house, she saw mares and foals cantering around the fields soon to belong to Jack Trevelyan, kicking up their feet, enjoying the warm spring weather. Campions and bluebells lined the hedges now, where primroses had already flowered in February and March.

Her mother had collected Aunt Nell from the train yesterday, and the two women were busy in the kitchen putting the finishing touches to a mouth-watering assortment of dishes. Kate gave her aunt a hug.

'Where's Pa?' she asked.

'He and Jeff are up at the stables,' her mother said. 'Hurry up and take them away. The weather is so wonderful today, not even a breath of wind. Nell and I have decided to have the buffet on the terrace and I want to start putting up the tables soon.'

Kate ran her finger around the edge of a bowl that her mother had used to make chocolate and rum mousse.

'Mmm yummy.'

'I've made two, so there'll be plenty for you later. Go now, or they'll be back looking for you!'

Kate, laughing, was pushed unceremoniously out of the door.

Jeff and Kate managed to keep their father out riding for the rest of the morning. So by the time they had hung up the tack, rubbed down the horses and turned them out in a nearby paddock it was nearly twelve thirty.

'Just time for a quick shower before lunch,' her father said. 'I'm feeling quite peckish after the ride. Hope there is something interesting for lunch.'

Kate looked at her brother and they shared a smile.

A few very close friends of her father had been invited to come early, and they were out on the terrace nursing drinks when her father emerged later to a rousing welcome.

There was no doubting the surprise and delight on his face, and Kate was happy for him. If Daniel did turn up she hoped it would be possible to keep him well away from her father, and get him to leave without a fuss. This was, after all, Pa's day.

Nell and her mother were busy bringing the food out from the kitchen, so Kate lent a hand. A whole salmon covered with thin half-circle slices of cucumber to represent scales, then painted with aspic, sat beside small tartlets of chicken and asparagus covered with a lemon mayonnaise dressing. There was a large rib of beef on the bone and leg of pork. A tray of thick wedges of melon, three kinds of salad, and French loaves which her mother always insisted on baking herself.

Pride of place went to the goose, which had been boned to make carving easy and stuffed with two kinds of stuffing. Kate was delighted with the puddings; the chocolate and rum mousses and an enormous Tarte Tatin, which was her mother's speciality. It consisted of cooked apple slices in caramel on a bed of pastry.

More guests were arriving every minute. Carrying out a cheese-board that wouldn't have disgraced the local delicatessen, she anxiously scanned the new arrivals, but there was no sign of Daniel.

'Time for you to go and change, Kate,' her mother said, as they passed in the hall. 'If your friend arrives before you get back, I'll look after him.'

Kate knew her mother was right. She couldn't stay in her riding gear all day, but worried that, if he did come, someone would talk to Daniel before she did, she raced upstairs and showered and dressed in minutes.

Her heart-shaped face had the golden blush of a new tan and she needed only the lightest make-up to make the most of her flawless complexion. A quick brush to smooth her hair back in style and she was ready.

Out on the terrace again she mingled with her father's friends, stopping to chat half-heartedly here and there, her eyes always searching the crowd. Sally, glass in one hand and a plate in the other, walked over.

'Hi. Any sign of him yet?'

'No. He probably won't turn up,' Kate said, unable to decide whether to be pleased or

30

sorry if he didn't.

'I wouldn't be too sure, if I were you. Anyway, who's that gorgeous creature your mother's talking to?' Sally enquired, gesturing with her glass to a point behind Kate's back. I'm sure I would have remembered if I'd seen him before.'

Kate turned around and her heart skipped a beat. She saw her mother standing a little apart from the crowd, deep in conversation with Daniel Ashcroft.

Too late now to drag him away from the party without anyone seeing him, as she had hoped to do. Kate's worst fears had been realised and she knew that the only thing what would help her right now was a miracle.

'So, he came,' Kate whispered, watching Daniel's self-assured and easy manner, his head thrown back in laughter at something her mother was saying. He looked so full of life and vitality, she could have watched him all day she thought, walking over to join them.

'Hello, Kate. You look beautiful today,' he said, as she came to a halt. He lifted her hand to his lips and kissed it, squeezing it before he released her.

Her mother turned, her glance registering the jade shirt and trousers and the pink flush suffusing her daughter's skin. She smiled approvingly.

'There you are, darling. As you can see, Mr Ashcroft and I—'

'Daniel, please, Mrs Hamilton.'

Kate looked at her mother apprehensively. Francine now knew who he was, but how was she going to react? She needn't have worried. Francine, the perfect hostess as always, seemed to have taken it in her stride.

'Thank you, Daniel. Kate, you must take him to meet our friends and also your papa. Daniel has a present for him. Oh, and make sure you give him some food before it all vanishes. I'll see you later,' she said, moving away.

Kate glanced at the bottle in his hand and noticed it was malt whisky.

'What's that saying about not trusting Greeks bearing gifts?'

Daniel laughed. 'I want to impress him.'

'Oh, I think you'll manage that!' Kate asked. In more ways than one, she added to herself. Now that her mother had spoken to Daniel it would be impossible for her to spirit him away without questions being asked.

Kate's heart sank as they walked across the lawn to where her father stood deep in conversation with some friends. This was the very thing Kate had tried to avoid, introducing her father to his sworn enemy's step-son, but there was no way out of it now. Oh, well, here we go, she thought, pulling Daniel into the group surrounding her father.

'Pa, I'd like you to meet—'

Her father turned, a smile on his face. 'Ah,

you must be the young man my wife told me would be coming. Met Kate on the plane, I hear?'

'Yes, that's right. Happy birthday,' Daniel said, shaking hands and handing over the bottle of whisky.

David Hamilton looked at the label. 'My dear boy, what a lovely surprise! I'll enjoy drinking this. Thank you.'

Kate, realising that her father still didn't know the name of their visitor, and unable to believe her luck, grabbed Daniel's arm and pulled hard. 'Sorry to dash, Pa, but we haven't had anything to eat yet.'

David Hamilton looked at his daughter in surprise. 'Oh . . . right. Well, we'll catch up with each other later then,' he said, as Daniel was dragged unceremoniously away.

'Don't you think that was a bit rude?' Daniel asked later, piling food on to two plates, while Kate, weak with relief, gathered together some cutlery and a couple of glasses of wine and tried not to spill any.

'Not in the circumstances.'

Daniel raised an eyebrow. 'Don't you think you'd better explain?'

'Not now. Food first, talk later,' she said, perching on top of a low stone wall at the edge of the terrace and biting into a chicken and asparagus tart as if her life depended on it.

She looked up. 'Oh, bother. Don't look now, my brother's heading this way!'

Jeff and Sally were introduced to Daniel by a somewhat reluctant Kate. After an initial coolness the two men got on well, an unspoken understanding seeming to pass between them. Kate gratefully let the conversation ebb and flow around her until she heard her brother say, '. . . thought she was sickening for something. Now I know differently. Normally when I call her Pudding she thumps me.'

Kate suddenly remembered Jeff calling her by her pet name when he collected her from the airport on Friday. She punched him on the arm and everyone laughed. 'Will you stop that!'

'Why "Pudding"?' Daniel asked.

'Don't you dare, Jeff Hamilton! I'll never speak to you again.'

'Peace at last,' he said, tweaking her cheek. It's obvious, really. She can't refuse a pudding. Never could, even when she was little. She has to eat two. When we go out she looks at the pudding trolley before deciding what main course to eat.'

Kate wanted to die with embarrassment. 'Jeff, you're awful. Take him away, Sally. Find a big hole and drop him in it.'

Sally linked her arm through Jeff's. 'Come on, Trouble, I think you've caused enough mischief for one day.'

Later, to her undying humiliation, Daniel refused to believe Kate when she said she didn't want a dessert, promptly going off to

34

find her some.

He came back with two large plates, full of puddings and surmounted by large dollops of Cornish cream. She sighed, defeated. Daniel picked up a spoon and started to eat his mousse.

'I can quite understand,' he said with a straight face, 'how a person could easily become addicted to puddings!'

Kate scowled at him and kept eating. When they had finished he took her hand in both of his, turned it over, palm uppermost, and began tracing circles with a fingertip.

He looked up at her suddenly, catching her unawares, his eyes darkening as he gazed into hers.

'I think it's talking time,' he said. 'Come on.' He pulled her to her feet and they started to walk away from the house.

'Kate, what if—'

'Daniel, I must—'

They both started to talk at once, but were interrupted by a shout from behind them.

'Stop!'

Kate turned around to see her father almost running across the lawn towards them. Although David Hamilton was only five foot six he was a strongly-built, powerful man. He looked furious, that much was obvious. He came to a halt in front of them.

'Just what is the meaning of this, Kate?' he demanded. 'I want an explanation, and I want

35

it now!'

His face was puce, and she could see a vein throbbing on his temple. 'Pa, whatever—'

'Don't give me any excuses, my girl! You know who you invited here today. You deliberately brought a member of that family to my house. A Trevelyan . . . here . . . '

'But I didn't—' Kate began.

Daniel took her hand in his and gave it a reassuring squeeze. 'My name is Ashcroft, Mr Hamilton. Although my mother married a Trevelyan I am not related to him, and surely should be judged on my own merit? Although I have to say that if circumstances were different I would be very proud to be his son. Kate had no idea who I was when she invited me.'

Kate saw her father bunch his hands into fists and move menacingly towards Daniel, his agitation increasing.

'I don't give a damn what you call yourself, you're the same family. Get off my property now, and stay off!'

CHAPTER THREE

Daniel was already speaking again. 'Naturally, if I'm not a welcome guest here I shall leave. I'm sorry you feel that way. We were just going across to Polventon Manor to look at the plans for the hotel, weren't we, Kate? So we'll be going now.' He tucked her arm under his and gripped it firmly.

'Is this true?' her father asked.

All this was news to Kate but, she decided on impulse, surely it would be better if someone actually found out what the Trevelyans were up to? And why shouldn't it be her? Besides, it would be a good opportunity to put her father's side of the case to Daniel. She took a deep breath.

'Well . . . yes.'

Her father gave her a withering look, turned around and strode off.

Daniel, virtually marching her across the grass, said, 'I haven't got a clue where we are heading.'

'Oh . . . yes, this is OK,' Kate said, rapidly unscrambling her thoughts and taking her bearings. She had known her father would be mad when he found out who Daniel was, but the intensity of his anger had surprised her.

'We can take the short-cut through the copse and across our fields—sorry, your fields, I suppose I should say. And for goodness' sake, slow down, I can't keep up.'

He matched his stride to hers, his grip on her arm still tight. 'You're out of condition.'

'I'm no such thing! Besides, these aren't exactly the shoes for a cross-country run,' Kate said, leaning a hand against a tree, and inspecting the heels of her now grass-stained sandals.

They walked at a more sedate pace through the copse, a picture now with a carpet of bluebells under the low-canopied trees. Daniel came to a stop at the river and Kate sat down on the short, springy turf.

'You OK?' he asked, lowering himself to sit beside her.

She nodded and looked out towards the water where a heron, picking its way carefully in the shallows, was looking for an afternoon snack.

Kate knew she had to ask some important questions before they went any further.

'Daniel,' she said, avoiding his gaze.

'Mmm?'

'Did you know who I was? On the plane?'

He took a moment or two to answer her and when he did his voice was soft. 'Yes, Kate, I did.'

'Then why did you still—'

'But I didn't know everything,' he interrupted. 'Jack told me there was a David Hamilton renting some of Polventon's land, and I knew the name of your father's property, of course, so obviously you had to be his daughter. But I had no idea that there was such animosity between the two of them.' He took her hand in his. 'You have to believe me, Kate. When I met you I just liked what I saw and wanted the opportunity to get to know you better. When you invited me here, it seemed like the ideal opportunity.'

Kate felt a warm glow steal over her as Daniel continued.

'I've tackled Jack several times about the set-up here since you and I met, but he was always evasive. I put it down to him being so worried about my mother. She hasn't been well lately.'

'No, so we heard. I'm sorry,' Kate said.

'Thanks. Anyway, it wasn't until your mother told me what to expect—'

Kate swung her head round to look at him. 'Hang on. My mother told you?'

'Yes. When I arrived she asked me if I knew how things stood. When she saw I didn't know what she was talking about, she filled me in.'

'But how did she know who you were?'

'She said she put two and two together on Friday night.'

Kate broke off a blade of grass and chewed thoughtfully the end of it. So her mother had known all along.

'Goodness knows what the row between your father and Jack was about, Kate,' Daniel said, 'but it doesn't have anything to do with us.'

'Except now my father has to give up the land which he has rented for years, for your hotel, and his business is going to suffer. He sees this as a deliberate move by your step-father to ruin him.'

'You can't honestly believe—'

39

'I don't know what to think,' Kate cut in, absentmindedly pulling up tufts of grass. 'Why can't you let him buy the land? You can't possibly need it all!'

Daniel sighed. 'We want our guests to be able to walk down here, Kate. Later we may even have a dinghy or two on the river for their use. We also need the land for privacy. This is going to be an upmarket hotel and we want to make the most of the country setting.' Daniel shook his head. 'You must see that this isn't a personal vendetta.'

She shrugged her shoulders. 'The wildlife is bound to suffer,' she said, pointing to where the heron had now been joined by two of his companions. 'We've got a badger sett in the copse, too. What will happen to them when their peace is destroyed by people who don't understand them, or even care?'

'The type of guests who are going to stay at Polventon aren't likely to be environmental vandals. Quite the opposite, I would think.'

'Hmm . . . but you can't guarantee that, can you?' Kate insisted.

Daniel gave an exasperated sigh and ran a hand through his hair.

'Nothing is guaranteed in this life, Kate, as you well know, but I'm certainly going to do my best to keep this small part of the world as near to nature as possible. Does that make you feel better?'

She nodded, wanting to believe him, but not

totally convinced. 'OK.'

Daniel smiled. 'Friends again?' He turned her face towards him and, leaning over, kissed the corner of her mouth. 'Now, let's get going,' he said, briskly, standing up and pulling her to her feet, 'we've got lots to see.'

He kept her hand in his, and they walked in companionable silence over the fields to Polventon Manor.

The five acres of formal garden were flourishing. The camellias were over, but the rhododendrons and azaleas made giant splashes of colour over the parkland, and the sturdy bases of oak trees sheltered large clumps of daffodil leaves which were dying back, having flowered their hearts out in March and April. Lawns were trimmed and herbaceous borders were getting ready to wear their summer clothes.

The large Georgian house stood four-square to the elements. The north elevation with its front door and double-pillared portico faced the drive, the views from the south-facing windows were all of the river.

Daniel stopped to take it all in, gazing round with interest. 'He must have loved his garden. It's in the most terrific condition,' he said.

Kate nodded. 'Yes, this was his pride and joy. He had two part-time helpers, but did most of it himself. I think virtually all his time and money went on its upkeep.'

A black Jaguar saloon was parked at the front of the house. From a passenger seat Daniel took a roll of plans.

'I left the car here earlier and walked across to your parents' place,' he said, going towards the front door of the manor house and pulling a long key from his pocket. He unlocked the door. 'Come on in.'

They walked into the large entrance hall and were greeted by a musty smell. A wide, solid-oak staircase wound its way to the first floor, the floors which were visible were also made of wood. Ornate plaster mouldings around the doors had intricate designs carved on them, but the house had been sadly neglected. It showed in the worn-out furniture, the threadbare carpets and a number of different-sized rectangles of bright wallpaper where pictures had obviously once hung.

Daniel gestured towards them. 'Money problems, do you think?'

'Yes. I've seen the paintings go, one by one. When he ran short of money he sold another. It's a tragedy, really,' Kate said. 'Pa bought the home farm from him after his wife died fourteen years ago. Since then it's been just him and the garden. He was a lovely old boy.'

They wandered from room to room to get the feel of the house. Dust-sheets covered the larger pieces of furniture in many of the upstairs rooms.

'We bought some of the furniture, and the

rest is being moved this coming week,' Daniel said. 'Then we can start on the work. Had they lived here long?'

Kate nodded, running a finger along the dust-covered top of a Georgian snap-table. 'Yes. This has been in the colonel's family since it was built in the late seventeen hundreds. He was the last of the direct line. No children though, very sad. I think he just gave up when his wife died.'

'Come and look at these,' he said, beckoning her over.

Kate walked to where Daniel stood at a desk, unrolling the plans for the renovations. His enthusiasm for the project was infectious, and Kate soon came to realise, listening to him talk, that the work was going to be handled sensitively.

'We're only having eight large bedrooms on the first floor, each with their own bathroom—two bathrooms in one case—and two small suites on the second floor.' He named a well-known interior designer who would be coming to mastermind the interiors.

He bent over the plans, his shoulder almost touching Kate's. She was having trouble concentrating on what he was saying to her, too busy watching his strong, tanned hands moving over the plans. Breathing suddenly became difficult for her.

'So, what do you think . . . ?'

'Sorry? I missed that.'

43

Daniel shot her an amused glance. 'I said, as this is a conservation area we weren't allowed to put up any new buildings, so we're going to convert the carriage-house and the stables into a leisure area. Swimming-pool, solarium, sauna, gym, that sort of thing. Look at this . . . ' He put an arm around her shoulder and drew her closer.

'Now, the gun room and the butler's pantry are going to be—' He turned his head slowly towards her and gently kissed her cheek. Kate gave a small moan of delight. 'You're not listening to a word I'm saying, are you?'

'No.'

He tilted her face upwards and lowered his head to hers. She closed her eyes. It was a gentle kiss, yet sensual and exciting. She smiled dreamily, wanting this moment to go on for ever.

'Just think, none of this would have happened if you had been at the hotel when I phoned on Saturday.'

'Oh?'

'Well . . . I phoned to try and put you off coming today, when I realised who you were, but you weren't at the hotel. If you had been, we wouldn't be here now.'

He smiled. 'But I was.'

A frown tugged at her brow, 'I don't understand.'

'Simple.' He smiled smugly. 'I told our receptionist to say I couldn't be contacted till

Monday. I had an idea you might try to put me off.'

His words shocked Kate. She pushed against him in an effort to disentangle herself, but he held her arms in a firm grip.

'Why?' Kate asked, as her emotions swung wildly from elation to devastation.

'I told you, I liked what I saw and wanted to get to know you better.'

'But we still could have done that, and have avoided that scene with Pa.'

Daniel sighed, lowered his hands and moved away from her. 'Kate, would you still have come out with me knowing who I was?'

She tried to give him an honest answer. 'I don't know, but—'

'That's my answer.'

Kate crossed to the window, shivering despite the warmth of the sun streaming through it. She looked out, unseeing, at the well-tended gardens and the river beyond.

Her mind raced. He had already admitted that he knew who she was on the plane. He had been quite happy to be introduced to her father and had even wanted an explanation when she dragged him away while they were still speaking. The malt whisky was obviously to soften the shock when her father discovered who he was. What was he up to?

'You expect me to believe that was your reason for coming? You came over especially to see my father, didn't you? You must have thought it was your lucky day,' she said, disgustedly, 'when my invitation paved the way.

'I suppose you wanted to see if my father was going to cause any trouble over the grazing. He's going to lose business and money by giving the fields back, but that doesn't worry you, does it? You don't care about anything but your damned hotel!'

Daniel raked a hand distractedly through his hair. 'Kate, sweetheart, please believe me when—'

'Don't, "Kate, sweetheart" me!' she shouted. 'You're a fine pair, you and your step-father! And to think I actually wanted to believe you.'

He moved towards her, but she ran out of the room and down the stairs, her heels tapping furiously on the wooden floors. She pulled open the front door and raced across the lawn. Climbing over white-painted post-and-rail fences she startled mares and foals as she ran, taking the shortest route home.

Her flight was drastically halted in the copse when the heel of her sandal caught in the undergrowth and sent her flying, knocking the wind from her. When, eventually, she raised her head to look round she was watched by a silent drift of bluebells.

Kate was reminded of how happy she had been when she saw them last, little more than an hour ago. The memory sent a sharp stab of

46

pain through her and she laid her head on her arms and groaned.

Well, at least I've got some more information for Pa, Kate remembered thankfully, when she finally pulled herself together and sadly made her way back to her parents' house. Perhaps the day hadn't been totally wasted.

CHAPTER FOUR

The day after the party Kate had been out shopping during a quiet spell in the shop. The expedition hadn't been so much to buy anything in particular, more an excuse to have something to occupy her mind, but it failed to work.

She left a small package in one of the large multiples and only became aware of it when a sales assistant had run after her to return it. When she bumped into a second shopper while not looking where she was going she decided she would be less of a menace in the shop than on the streets.

She passed the cathedral and turned into a narrow, cobbled street. The sight of the little street always lifted Kate's spirits, and today was no exception. It had recently been pedestrianised, which made for more pleasant browsing and shopping. Water splashed along

47

gulleys between pavement and cobbles, the sun bouncing off the tumbling water like sparklers in a firework display.

The street was looking a picture. Hanging baskets hung from shop walls and lamp-posts, their flowers a riot of cascading colour. A flower shop whose pots of flowers were spread out on to the pavement displayed hot-house roses next to elegant ice-blue spikes of delphiniums, and a bucket of gypsophila was trying to spread its tiny white flowers into a container of yellow daisies.

The fine weather was holding, and the sun reflected from the newly-washed black paintwork of Kate's shop. The single word *Hamiltons* was depicted in gold along the top of the double-fronted façade.

Inside, Sally smiled smugly and indicated to a large bunch of spring flowers which had been delivered to the shop in Kate's absence.

'They're for you,' she said.

Kate took the card from its small envelope and read, *My apologies for yesterday. Let's start again. How about dinner on Friday night, eight o'clock? Daniel.*

Kate promptly tore the card up and gave the flowers to Sally to take home.

'But why?' Sally said, burying her nose amongst the freesias and tulips.

Kate smiled wistfully at her friend. 'It seems I wasn't the main attraction after all. This is just another attempt to get at Pa through me.'

48

The day dragged by for Kate, in spite of being busy. Sally had repeatedly tried to get her to change her mind, but Kate refused to discuss it.

Work, which normally had a calming influence on her, failed to ease her warring emotions and sleep was almost non-existent.

Dark circles peered back at her from her mirror and she had to wear more than her usual amount of make-up to cover them before Sally noticed, and started asking her difficult questions.

Her mind had re-run the events of Sunday until her head buzzed. Every conversation with Daniel had been turned over and dissected until she didn't know what to think any more.

*   *   *

On Wednesday morning, Kate returned to the shop after delivering a small order to one of her shop-keeping neighbours. Lifting the brass door latch and walking in, she was shocked to find the man responsible for her sleepless nights leaning against the counter talking to Sally, laughing at something she had just said.

He was wearing a beautifully-cut, dark-blue business suit, the jacket fitting his powerful shoulders like a glove, and to Kate's hungry eyes he looked good enough to eat.

'Good morning, Kate.'

'Oh . . . hello there,' she said, wondering at

49

the reason for his visit. Had he discovered that her father had managed a meeting with the colonel's Canadian relative? Although the Canadian had been very sympathetic, he had told her father what the family already knew, that the property was sold and he was only in this country to arrange the transfer of the money and to clear out the house. He had suggested that they approach Trevelyan direct.

She eyed him warily, but his words surprised her.

'I've come in for a bottle of wine for my mother. Sally told me you were the expert and, as you weren't going to be long, I waited.'

Kate sent Sally a jaundiced look. 'She sells herself short. Sally is quite capable of recommending a good wine, when she wants to.'

Sally had the grace to blush.

'Although, with the stocks you must keep at the hotel it seems odd that you would need to come here for anything.'

One eyebrow rose enquiringly.

'Sorry,' Kate said, taking a deep breath and trying to reign in her temper, 'that was uncalled for. You're very welcome. Have you got anything particular in mind?' She pinned a smile on her face, hoping it bore some semblance of normality.

His eyes twinkled and Kate saw him struggle to hold back a laugh.

'Yes, Kate, I've got something very special

in mind, but, for the wine, I want something different from our hotel stock. She's taking an interest in food again and the doctor says a small amount in moderation would be fine. Not white, though, she finds it too acidic.'

'How about a nice bottle of Burgundy?'

'Trust a woman to say that. Don't they always prefer burgundy to claret?'

Kate bit down angrily on a retort. 'That's not strictly true,' she said, heatedly, unable to stop herself rising to the bait he threw. 'I can appreciate a bottle of claret, like most people. You aren't going to drag me into that old argument.'

Daniel laughed. 'Looks like you fell right in it!'

Kate swallowed hard on her temper and wondered at his ability to wind her up so easily.

'I only suggested burgundy because, as a rule, it has a softer taste, not so much tannin as claret and, as your mother has been ill, she might prefer a more gentle wine.'

His expression sobered, and he nodded in agreement. 'Point taken. So, what do you have?'

They spent the next half-hour looking at Kate's stock of burgundies, discussed the merits of Australian Chardonnay against French and had a heated argument on which they thought best, champagne which had been made with red and white grapes, or only white,

51

which, in Kate's view, had more finesse and delicacy.

The time flashed by and Kate found herself enjoying every minute. She stopped talking and gazed at him for a while in silence.

'A penny for them, Kate.'

'It's unusual . . . finding a man who doesn't think it odd for a woman to be having this kind of discussion.'

'Don't men of your acquaintance find all this interesting?' He gestured to the surrounding racks of wine.

She looked down at the floor, and answered softly, 'No. Or, if they do, they don't like to admit it.'

'That's their loss, then, isn't it?' he commented.

Kate's thoughts immediately went to Paul, with whom she had worked in Bristol. Even he had found it hard to swallow. They started as friends and colleagues and had been going out together for two years before she came home to Cornwall to start her own business.

Kate flashed a look Daniel's way. He was certainly no Paul. He held her gaze for what seemed like an eternity, his sea-blue eyes mesmerising her—eyes to drown in.

Kate, delighted by his attitude, but embarrassed in case she had revealed too much about herself, began to move away. I could really fall for a man like this, came the unbidden thought. She pulled herself up with a start. This was dangerous thinking, indeed. It was enough that she found herself liking and respecting him, without adding any further complications.

If Daniel sensed her withdrawal, he didn't show it. He took two bottles of the burgundy they finally agreed on, and paid Sally, who wrapped them in sheets of tissue paper before putting them in a small carrier bag in the shop's colours of gold on black.

Kate gave him a tour of her stock-rooms.

'I'm very impressed, Kate. You've got an efficient, professional set-up here and plenty choices of wines.'

She glowed in the warmth of his approval. 'It hasn't always been easy.'

'I can imagine. Starting a business is never easy. Are you having difficulties now, like so many others?'

'Luckily, no. Pa helped me out so I wouldn't have to start with an overdraft. If I did have any large loans right now I would be very worried.'

Kate remembered, ruefully, what her friends and acquaintances had thought of it at the time. She had gone overnight, in their estimation, from being a nice girl to being a 'little rich kid'. Paul couldn't bear to think that she was being set up by her father, either, and that he would probably have to spend the rest of his life working for someone else.

Although Paul had wanted them to get

engaged, Kate knew that the feelings she had towards him were not sufficiently strong enough for marriage, and he hadn't been too thrilled when Kate refused to get involved on an intimate level. It had heralded the end of their relationship.

Since then, all her energy had gone into building up her business, and none of the men she met had been prepared to accept cancelled dates while she worked late. Nor did they think it very feminine for a woman to be a wine merchant. In their view, sometimes forcibly stated, they considered it men's work, and it damaged their egos to think that a woman could know more about wines and spirits than they did.

Kate had learned never to talk about it with anyone these days, which amazed her to find he was discussing it with Daniel.

'He helped Jeff, too. Did you know, he made over the farm to Jeff when he was twenty one?'

'No, I didn't.'

Kate showed him into her tiny office. With Daniel in it, it seemed even smaller.

'Pa says we have to make a success of our lives purely by our own efforts. He's helped us to start, but now we're on our own. He's very independent himself, you know.'

Daniel perched on the edge of her desk. 'So I'm discovering. Pig-headed was the way Jack described him. Look,' he said, running a hand through his hair, 'the real reason I'm here is that I've discussed your father's problem with Jack.'

Kate opened her mouth, but he held up a hand to silence her. 'Before you say anything, I've only mentioned the grazing and the problems your father will have when he loses it. If you're annoyed with me for speaking out of turn I'm sorry. I don't even know if it will do any good, but I had to try.'

Kate was overwhelmed. In spite of the way she had treated Daniel he had gone out of his way to speak to his step-father knowing how the two men felt about each other. Kate's eyes shone as she looked up at him. 'I . . . I don't know what to say. After Sunday—'

'Don't say anything,' he interrupted. 'How about our dinner on Friday? Is it still on?'

Kate's pulse raced with excitement. He really does want to see me again, she thought, and this time I won't make a hash of it. She smiled. 'I'd like that.'

'Good. I'll pick you up at about eight.' He moved around her desk and kissed her cheek. 'Till Friday, then.'

Collecting the bottles of wine on his way through the shop, he said goodbye to Sally and strode purposefully out.

Kate folded her arms and hugged herself delightedly as she watched him go. Sally smiled smugly at her, with an 'I told you so' expression on her face.

'Don't you dare say anything!' Kate said warningly.

'Who? Me?'

Kate gave a good impression of the Cheshire Cat. Friday seemed like an awfully long way away.

*   *   *

Her father lost his temper when she told him what Daniel had said.

'What business is it of his?' David Hamilton shouted as he paced his study, his short, stocky body radiating anger. 'There was no need for you to have had anything to do with him. I understand that you didn't know who he was when you invited him on Sunday, but I don't want any favours from that family.'

Kate perched on the edge of his desk, swinging her legs. 'But, Pa, I thought you would have been delighted that someone was taking an interest in your problem. He might even be able to help. Who knows, he could talk Jack into letting you keep the land.'

'A Trevelyan? Help? You must be joking! The only people they are likely to help are themselves.'

'How many times do I have to tell you that he's not a Trevelyan?' Kate argued, beginning to get annoyed with her father.

He came to a halt, lifted his shoulders and his hands, the palms upwards. 'So? What's in a

56

name, They're the same family, whatever they're called.'

Pushing his hands in the pockets of his trousers and rocking backwards and forwards on his heels he said, 'Where did you see him, anyway?'

Kate picked up an antique silver and ivory calendar from the desk and idly turned it over in her hands. 'He came into the shop yesterday.'

'Huh! Spying!'

'No, he wasn't.' Kate felt her normally even temper begin to fray. 'He came in to get a couple of bottles of red for his mother.'

'Oh, yes?' Her father came over to her and peered into her face, his own suffused with anger. 'Hotel run out, has it?'

Kate blushed at the reminder of her own accusation and looked away. 'You know very well it hasn't. He wanted something special. He also wanted to tell me about Jack.'

'And?' He resumed his pacing.

'And nothing.' Kate wasn't about to tell her father, or anyone, about the date with Daniel. She rubbed a hand over her face, and sighed wearily. 'Pa, you've got to stop acting like this. You know your blood pressure won't stand it. Besides, Daniel might do some good.'

Her father stopped pacing and, with his back to the window, said, 'You don't know what the Trevelyans are like.'

Kate eased herself off the desk and moved

towards her father. 'Then for goodness' sake, tell me. You've had this silly feud going on for as long as I can remember, and you don't even talk about it. If you did, you might find it helped to clear the air—put it in perspective.'

'I'm not discussing it, except to say that in business the Trevelyans are ruthless. They don't care who they step on to get where they want, and if you want my advice, you'll stay out of their way.'

CHAPTER FIVE

Friday arrived, even busier than usual, and the phone rang non-stop. Kate illogically expected every call to be Daniel and was disappointed when they turned out not to be. She had spent hours the previous evening deciding what to wear for her date, settling on something one minute and rejecting it again the next, and had passed the best part of the morning working on automatic pilot, while her thoughts were all of Daniel.

'Where ever have all these orders come from?' Sally asked as they grabbed a late-morning cup of coffee. 'This is the busiest day we've had for weeks.'

Kate smiled at her friend. 'Don't knock it, Sally, it's good for business. Here, get your energy levels up, have a biscuit.' She handed

Sally the open packet of biscuits.

'Thanks. Look, I've been thinking. There's a lot of work here with all these extra orders, so I'm going to stay for an hour or two after we close this evening and help out.'

'But, Sally—'

'No—just listen,' she said, waving a biscuit around in the air. 'Sam will be fine staying longer with Mum and at least we can have the majority of them boxed and ready for delivery in the morning. Besides,' she said smugly, 'we can't have you missing your date, can we?'

'That would be marvellous, Sally, thanks. I'm not going to be silly enough to refuse an offer like that. It's going to be a rush tomorrow as it is, especially with the two wedding orders to go out first thing. At least I've only got to make the ice cubes for the champagne buckets for those.'

The phone rang again and the two girls groaned. 'My turn,' Sally said, heading for the office.

'Switch on the ice-machine when you pass, will you?'

'Will do,' Sally called over her shoulder as she hurried to the phone.

Kate had just finished serving another customer when Sally came out of the office, face white and drawn, walking as if in a trance.

'Good grief, whatever's wrong?' Kate hurried to her friend's side, put an arm around her shoulder and led her back into the office.

59

Sally was shaking, so Kate sat her down on a chair.

'That was Mum,' her friend sobbed. 'It's Sam. He—he ran out into the road while he was playing and was knocked down by a car. The ambulance has just arrived, and they're going to hospital.'

'Oh, Sally—you've got to go to him at once.' Kate brought her face down to Sally's level. 'Nothing is as important as Sam. Your place is with him right now.'

Sally took a handkerchief from her pocket, blew her nose and took a deep breath. 'I'll be fine. It's just the shock, but I'll cope. Anyway, I must stay. Who's going to help you with making up the orders so you can go out with Daniel tonight?'

'That's not a problem. Do you feel up to driving?' Sally nodded.

Kate fished around in her handbag for her car keys and gave them to her friend. 'Good. Take my car. My insurance will cover you to drive it, but for goodness' sake be careful. We don't want you ending up in hospital with him.'

Sally gave her a watery smile and a hug.

'Give the little scamp a kiss from me,' Kate said, as she helped Sally into her coat, opened the back door and gave her a push in the direction of the garage.

As soon as Kate had seen Sally safely on her way to the hospital she phoned Jeff to tell him the bad news. She knew her brother would want to be with Sally at a time like this.

*   *   *

At the first opportunity she telephoned the retired gentleman who helped out three days a week with their deliveries. He was supposed to be on holiday this week, but if he was at home he would probably come in and lend her a hand for an hour or two, glad of some extra money. But her luck was out.

'He's gone fishing with some friends,' his widowed sister said, 'and won't be back until Saturday. Do you want to leave a message?'

Kate declined, and put down the phone with a heavy heart.

Although she had skirted lightly over the problem and given Sally the impression that she could cope, Kate knew that she was now in serious trouble. There was no possibility of Kate being in the shop and doing the orders, let alone making the deliveries tomorrow as well.

At five thirty Kate locked the shop and put the 'Closed' sign up with relief. She could feel a headache forming and wondered, idly, if a storm was brewing. The day had been very close and muggy.

She walked slowly back to the office and sat down, her elbows on the desk.

Putting her head in her hands she circled her temples with her fingers. Problems weren't new to Kate, and she loved the discipline of thought and logic necessary to solve them, but what depressed her tonight was the knowledge that she must cancel her date with Daniel.

He was becoming special to her. She toyed with the idea of asking him to come over for a meal at the flat when she had finished for the evening, but one look at the sheaf of orders waiting to be filled was enough to make her realise that this idea was a non-starter.

He may also think it was rather forward of her to suggest it after such a short acquaintance. After all, this was only their second date, if you counted the disastrous party.

Not one to wallow in self-pity, she soon rallied. 'This won't do, Hamilton,' she said out loud. 'The sooner you start, the sooner you'll be finished.' She pulled a sheet of paper towards her and started writing.

The telephone bell cut through the silence. It was Jeff.

'Good news,' he said, his voice jubilant. 'Apparently Sam ran into the road and luckily just took a glancing blow from the car. He's badly bruised, but no bones broken, thank goodness. Young bodies are very resilient, aren't they? He's a very lucky boy.'

'Oh, Jeff, that's wonderful news. How is Sally?'

'In shock. Although I don't know who's worse, Sally or her mother. Sally blames herself for not being there, her mother blames herself for not looking out for him, and Sam is getting cheekier by the minute, ordering all the nurses around.'

Kate laughed and doodled some circles on her pad. 'Tell Sally she's not to worry about things here. I'll see her when she feels she can leave Sam, and not before.' She was glad he couldn't see her crossing her fingers.

'Thanks, Pudding, I'll make sure she knows that. I'm going to take them all home now. ' 'Bye.'

Kate put down the phone feeling much happier, delighted that at least there was one bright spot in the day. She made herself a cup of coffee and, with a sheaf of orders, went to the stockroom to start making them up.

Deep in her task she heard a rumble of thunder, and it reminded Kate that she hadn't phoned Daniel yet.

No time like the present, she thought, moving to her office and hunting through the telephone directory for the hotel number.

The receptionist was cheerful, but no, Mr Ashcroft wasn't in the hotel at the moment.

'Can I put you through to the flat?' she offered. 'He may very well be up there with the family.'

Kate agreed, and after a short wait was put through.

'I should like to speak to Daniel, if he's there,' Kate said politely.

'Who is this?' a snooty voice queried.

'Kate Hamilton.'

'That name sounds familiar. Oh, I know. Aren't you Daniel's little shop-keeper? I've heard him talk about you.'

Kate gasped, taken aback. Surely this couldn't be Daniel's mother?

'Is that Mrs Trevelyan?' she asked hesitantly.

'Of course not,' the voice said. 'This is Adele Forrester. I'm a friend of Daniel's. In fact, you could say I'm a very good friend of Daniel's.'

Kate felt her nails biting into the soft flesh of her palms, and bit down on an angry retort. She took a deep breath and tried again. 'Is he there?'

'No, sorry,' the voice said, sounding not in the least bit sorry. 'Can I give him a message?'

Not likely, Kate thought. Somehow she didn't think the message would be passed on unscrambled. 'Will he be back soon?'

'Oh, yes, quite soon. He'll have to be, we're going out this evening.'

An icy hand squeezed Kate's heart. She knew she had no claim on Daniel—how could she when they had only met such a short time ago—but to change his mind about their date and not even have the courtesy to phone and cancel it seem callous. This woman sounded as though she knew what Daniel was doing, and why would she lie? Kate's thoughts were in turmoil.

A squawk came from the phone. 'Are you still there?' the voice demanded.

'Yes,' Kate said, faintly.

'Well? Do you want to leave a message, or not?'

Kate had no choice. 'Umm—well, yes. We were supposed to be—' She cleared her throat and started again. 'Tonight we were—'

Kate didn't know what message to give, what words to say. This woman would only gloat over her humiliation and rejection if she knew that Kate had been stood up by Daniel. And stood up she most certainly had been, if Adele Forrester was telling the truth.

She heard the other woman laugh. 'Oh, I see—you mean you had an appointment with Daniel this evening?'

'Yes,' Kate confessed, grabbing at the straw offered.

'To talk about business, no doubt. And now you want to cancel it?'

'Yes. A—a previous engagement.'

'I shouldn't worry about it. He's obviously forgotten about it himself. I'll tell him, anyway, when he comes in,' the smug voice replied, and the call was disconnected.

The hand that replaced Kate's receiver was shaking. For almost half an hour she continued to sit at her desk, not seeing anything, wrapped up in her disappointment, devastated to realise that she had been growing too fond of a man that she could no longer respect.

How could I have been so blind, she thought sadly. To think I believed him when he said he wanted to get to know me better. He seemed to like me—I must have been wrong about that, too. She felt the cold steal into her bones, and shivered.

How he must have laughed at me behind my back, pretending to be interested in my business when he probably couldn't give a damn about it, or about me.

A loud rumble of thunder pierced her innermost thoughts, and she heard the first heavy splashes of rain falling in the deserted street as she moved, trance-like, out of her chair and back to the stockroom.

The first flash of lightning lit up the boxes and cases piled up to the ceiling. The cup of coffee she had made for herself had long since gone cold, and a skin had formed on the top. She eyed it distastefully.

Tomorrow was another day, and work had to go on. The orders certainly wouldn't wait. She pulled the next one towards her and started to tick off the items as she boxed them up, writing up the invoices as she went.

The storm raging outside matched the one in her heart. Kate worked doggedly on until, just before eleven o'clock, she finished the last one.

Checking all the doors to make sure they were locked, she emerged into the back yard.

Rain was still falling heavily. She tilted her head upwards and felt the cleansing water fall on to her face.

Each step was torture to her as she dragged herself slowly up the wrought-iron steps. Kate had never felt so physically and emotionally drained, the water running off her hair and soaking her to the skin before she could reach the safety of the flat.

Once inside, she pulled the wet clothes from her body and piled them into the linen basket in her bedroom. She reset her alarm for six o'clock. Some of the orders would have to be delivered before she opened the shop, especially the two weddings.

She briefly mopped at her wet hair with a towel, pulled back the duvet and fell into bed. Sleep swiftly claimed her. But not for long . . .

*   *   *

Struggling to the surface of her exhausted sleep, Kate opened one eye and peered at her bedside clock. It read just after two o'clock. Her head fell back on to the pillow as she tried to work out what had woken her.

It certainly wasn't the storm, her sleep-drugged mind deduced, as there was silence outside her open window except for the gentle fall of rain. And then she heard it. A muffled bang, followed by a scraping sound.

Perspiration stood out on her forehead, and

fear ran like a cold flame through her body. The sound was coming from the yard at the back of the shop. Kate knew, without doubt, that someone was trying to break in.

CHAPTER SIX

'Police,' Kate whispered to the emergency services operator, balancing the phone between her ear and her shoulder and pulling the belt of her towelling robe tighter around her waist.

She had not switched the lights on in her tiny flat for fear of disturbing whoever was downstairs, and by the time she was put through to the police operator she was shaking so much she could hardly talk.

She explained that she could hear noises and thought that someone was trying to break in to her wine shop. The police operator was calm, but sympathetic, and didn't waste time once Kate had given her the details she needed.

'We'll have someone over there as soon as possible, Miss Hamilton, but on no account are you to try to deal with it yourself,' she warned. 'He, or they, may be armed.'

'Thank you,' Kate said, lowering the telephone receiver to its rest and walking slowly back to her bedroom. Still in the dark, she dressed in sweater and trousers, and pushed her feet into a pair of canvas shoes.

She listened. No sounds were coming from below now. She moved silently from room to room, still unable to hear anything. Carefully opening a window, she leaned out. In the stillness the sound of a car passing in the distance could be heard. The air had a fresh, clean smell to it and Kate inhaled it greedily.

She stayed in the same position for a few minutes, her heightened awareness unable to pick out any sound from below. They must have gone, she calculated. The burglar alarm would have gone off automatically if they had broken in, so perhaps they couldn't force the door and gave up.

She decided to walk down to the bottom of the steps to see if everything was all right. The police were bound to arrive shortly, anyway.

Taking a torch from the kitchen she opened the door quietly and walked out, her canvas shoes making no noise as she moved stealthily down the wrought-iron steps towards the yard.

Looking up at the sky, she saw that there were no stars visible, and clouds obscured the moon, but her eyes were beginning to adjust to the darkness.

At the bottom of the stairs she looked around the yard, picking out the shapes of the building. It was then that she saw the open storeroom door. Her breath caught in her throat.

Situated between the garage and the main buildings, the storeroom served as a stowage place for odds and ends together with the innumerable cartons and cases in which the wines and spirits were delivered. Although joined to her office and the back of the wine shop, it had no direct access into the shop. Kate moved slowly towards it.

She could hear boxes being thrown about and someone muttering. She reached the door, took her torch out of her pocket and switched it on. As the beam swung around the room she clearly saw two men dressed in black, both wearing balaclavas, rummaging around in the empty boxes.

'What the—' the first man began, when he looked up and saw Kate.

'Quick—let's move it,' the other said.

Kate instinctively moved back as they hurtled towards her and their only means of escape.

The first man to reach the door gave Kate a colossal push which sent her flying. As she fell towards the ground she hit the back of her head on a wooden half-barrel filled with geraniums, and the torch went spinning out of her hand. The men ran out of the yard into the service road and disappeared.

The pain was excruciating. She tried to stand up, but the world was spinning around at an alarming rate, and she fell back to the concrete surface of the yard.

At that moment a car turned into the yard, its headlights blazing, picking out her hunched figure. A door slammed and she heard footsteps running towards her. Please, please, let this be the police, she sobbed.

A voice that she recognised said, 'Kate? What's going on, what's happened?'

'Daniel?' She couldn't believe her ears.

'Yes, it's me,' he said, his voice full of anxiety. He crouched down beside her, and she felt his strong arms going around her. 'Can you stand, do you think?'

She tried to shake her head, but it hurt too much. He swore under his breath.

She sobbed on an intake of breath, but nothing came out. He held her tighter, saying, 'OK, I'll do all the work, just lean on me.'

As he started to lift her another car screeched to a halt in the road and two uniformed policemen got out of it and ran towards them.

'That will be far enough, I think, sir,' the first one said, moving towards Daniel purposefully. He looked at Kate. 'Would I be right in thinking that you are Miss Katherine Hamilton?'

She cleared her throat and managed to croak 'Yes.'

He turned his gaze back to Daniel. 'And perhaps you would be good enough to tell us who you are, sir, and what you think you're doing?'

Daniel expelled an angry breath. 'Sergeant,' he retorted, noticing the three stripes on the man's uniform, 'what does it look like I'm doing? I arrived only seconds ago, to find Miss Hamilton on the ground and obviously in some pain. How did you get here so fast?'

He gently lifted Kate to her feet. 'Hang on, sweetheart, you're doing fine.'

Kate didn't need any second bidding. Still groggy, she clutched the heavy wool of his sweater. Rain trickled down her neck and she felt nauseous, the thumping in her head like the base beat of a rock band at full volume.

'We had an emergency call from Miss Hamilton to say that someone appeared to be breaking into her premises. We get here to find her, apparently, the victim of an assault, and you standing over her. You must agree that it doesn't look good.'

'No—' Kate said agitatedly from the shelter of Daniel's arms, 'He—he's only just arrived. Two men—pushed me over. I fell on to that barrel—' She shivered.

Daniel swung her up into his arms. 'Miss Hamilton is in shock and bruised. Before you ask her any more questions I want to get her inside,' he said, turning purposefully towards the steps.

'Oh, right. You take her on up. We'll have a look around here first and then, later, we could perhaps ask you some questions, Miss Hamilton?' the sergeant said, stepping towards

72

the storeroom door.

Daniel, holding her close, carried her up to the flat, careful to avoid bumping her too much. Kate put her arms around his neck and rested her face wearily on his shoulder.

'Daniel?'

'Mmm?'

'Thanks.'

She felt him smile.

'How come you're here?'

'Oh, pure coincidence really.' He shifted her to a more comfortable position.'

'Some coincidence—at two o'clock in the morning, hmm?'

Daniel pushed open the door and carried her inside, pushing down light switches with his elbow as they passed. 'Which way now?' he asked.

'Down the hall, last door on the left,' Kate said, muzzily aware that he was changing the subject. He might not want to talk about it, she mused, but I'm glad he turned up when he did, no matter what the reason.

He lowered her feet to her bedroom carpet. 'Can you stand up on your own?' She nodded. 'Right then. Let's get you out of these wet clothes and in to bed.'

Kate's eyes widened. 'I can manage perfectly well on my own, thank you,' she said in a voice which, even to her ears, sounded dreadfully prim.

He eyed her doubtfully. 'Are you sure?'

She nodded.

'OK. Two minutes, then I'll be back. I'm going to look for a towel. Your hair is soaking.'

She was standing shivering in a towelling robe, when he returned. He sat her down and began to roughly towel dry her hair.

'I'm quite capable of doing this myself you know,' she said. 'You make me feel like a five-year-old.'

He stood back and surveyed her. 'You look like one,' he said.

'Charming!' she retorted.

He laughed. 'Anyway, you probably haven't enough strength to do it.'

Kate had to admit that he was right, she did still feel very weak, but at least she had stopped shivering.

'Right, time we got you to bed, I think. Nightdress around anywhere?' he asked, looking at the bed.

'Yes. In the top drawer over there,' she said, pointing to a mahogany chest of drawers with brass handles.

She watched him rummage around for a second or two, pulling out a wildly extravagant creation of silk and lace, bought in a moment of sheer madness and never worn. Daniel turned around and came towards her clutching a handful of dark blue silk.

'Here we are, this should do. It's the only one I could see.' He pushed it into her outstretched hands. 'Get this on, I won't be a

74

minute,' he said as he left the room.

She eyed the nightdress suspiciously, but threw the robe aside and pulled the offending garment over her head. It settled over her hips and swirled around her feet.

Daniel chose that moment to reappear, a hot-water bottle in one hand and a mug in the other. He stopped abruptly, his face a picture of amazement.

'That is a nightdress?' he exclaimed, his eyes taking in every inch of the gown from the lace straps and low-cut, silk bodice to the wide band of lace which fitted snugly under her bust and finished at her waist. His eyes travelled on to the flowing, watery silk that joined the lace and which fell gently to her ankles.

The colour gave Kate's skin the look of porcelain, and turned her brown eyes tawny. A faint blush rose in colour turning her cheeks a fiery red.

She pulled her frame up to its full five foot six inches. Her hair still wet, she looked like Aphrodite rising from the sea.

A strangled gasp came from Daniel's throat and he quickly turned it into a cough.

'Well, what's wrong with it?' she demanded, embarrassment giving way to anger.

'Nothing—nothing at all,' he exclaimed. 'Hop into bed with this,' he said, handing her the hot-water bottle. 'I've warmed you some milk. Can you manage it?'

'I think so. I did feel ill earlier, but it's

passing now.'

'Good. I can't give you any pills for the headache, though, until the doctor sees you.' He put the mug down on her bedside table and plumped up her pillows.

'Doctor? Oh, but I don't think I want—'

He sighed. 'Be sensible, Kate. You've had a nasty fall and hit your head. You could be concussed for all we know. I found his name under "Doctor" in the small book next to your telephone. I hope that was right?'

Kate lay back on the pillows, fought a strong desire to burst into tears and lost. One rolled silently down her cheek. Daniel mopped at it with his handkerchief and gently kissed the spot where it had fallen. She looked at him and saw in his face . . . what? Compassion? Sympathy?

'Don't worry, Kate, the worst is over.'

There was a knock on the front door. 'That'll be the boys in blue. Do you feel up to seeing them now?'

'Yes, better get it over with, I suppose.'

When Daniel reached the door he turned and said, 'Oh, and if I were you I would stay tucked down in the bed. You don't want the Devon and Cornwall Constabulary's notebook to catch fire, seeing you in that sexy outfit, now do you?' Throwing her a lewd theatrical wink, he opened the door for the policeman.

Kate, blushing, wished there was something to hand to throw at him, but the sudden

76

movement made the demons inside her head resume their pounding, and she sunk gratefully back on to her pillows.

The police sergeant came in, sat down on the chair and opened his notebook. Kate shot a mutinous glance at Daniel who was trying to keep a straight face.

'Now, Miss Hamllton, it appears that only the storeroom has been broken into, but as far as we can see it just contains boxes and odds and ends, is that correct?'

'Yes, that's right. That must also explain why the burglar alarm didn't go off. They obviously hadn't tried the doors into the shop or the stockroom.'

'They had,' the sergeant said. 'There were signs, but luckily those doors open outwards, making it difficult for anyone to force an entry. We also noticed that your garage door is up, and the garage empty. Have they stolen your car?'

Kate explained about Sally. While she was talking she saw Daniel lever himself away from the wall on which he was leaning, push his hands in his pockets and stare intently a her, as if he had suddenly found a new and interesting specimen worthy of closer inspection. She wondered what she had said to make him look like that.

The policeman turned to look at Daniel. 'Right then, Mr Ashcroft, let's get your statement if we may.'

'Nothing much to tell you really,' Daniel started. 'I had been visiting friends for the evening and I was on my way home.' He looked embarrassed. 'It was just lucky that I passed when I did.'

'It certainly seems that way, sir.'

Kate attempted to sit up, the duvet crept lower and Daniel quirked an eyebrow at her and smiled. She glanced down to see what she was revealing and struggled down under the covers again.

'Go on.' She was surprised to find that she had spoken.

'Well,' he continued, looking at the sergeant, 'as I drove home I saw that man-hole covers had been lifted off with the force of the storm water and as Miss Hamilton's premises are at about the same street level, I thought I would pop along and see if she was having problems with the water. Flooding, you know.' He looked smug.

Kate eyed him suspiciously. What was he up to, she wondered.

'You were expected, then?' the policeman continued.

'Yes—'

'No—'

He looked from one to the other. 'Which one of you is right?'

'Not exactly expected, no, but I thought I might help out if she was in trouble.'

'Looks like you did, sir, doesn't it?'

'I drove along the service road and saw two men running out of the yard. They ran along to a white transit van parked near the end of the road and drove off. Unfortunately I didn't realise the significance of it until I drove in and found her.'

'Pity.' The sergeant wrote in his notebook for a few minutes, Kate and Daniel looking warily at each other. 'Right,' he finally said, 'I've got everything I need for now. I'll probably want to talk to you both again. Tomorrow we will get someone in to see if they can find any fingerprints in the storeroom. We've contacted a local locksmith to fix the lock. He'll be around soon.' He stood up. 'We'll see ourselves out. Good night.'

The grey-haired doctor arrived as the police were leaving, and Daniel went out with them, leaving the doctor with Kate. He bustled into the room and said in a hearty voice, 'And what have you been doing, young lady? Wrestling with burglars, so I hear.'

Kate talked while he examined the lump on her head, which now felt enormous, looked into her eyes, then gave her a thorough examination.

'Feel sick or dizzy?' he asked, putting his stethoscope back into his bag, and sitting on the bed.

'No, not now.'

'Any double vision?'

'No. I think I blacked out for a second or

two, and everything seemed to spin around for a while, but that's all.'

'Hmm, all the same, I think we should have you in for twenty four hours,' he replied, his fingers on her wrist, checking her pulse.

'What? Hospital?' Kate exclaimed in horror. 'Oh, no, definitely not.'

'But my dear girl—'

'No. I'm not going to hospital, I can't possibly!' She thought desperately of the orders downstairs waiting to go out tomorrow, and knew she couldn't let people down. Besides the normal replenishment orders there were also the two weddings. Hospital was not an option she would even consider.

Daniel came back in and heard the last remark.

Watching her closely he surprised her by asking, 'Is it really necessary, or could she stay here? Providing, of course, that someone stayed with her.'

Hope bubbled inside Kate and she looked at the doctor expectantly.

He smiled. 'I've known Kate since she was born. You don't need to tell me how stubborn she can get, when she's a mind to.'

He turned back to Kate. 'If you refuse to go there's nothing I can do about it,' he said, shaking a finger at her, 'but you must let me know immediately you feel dizzy or have double vision. Is that clear?'

He looked at Daniel. 'You seem a sensible

young man. Can you guarantee me that someone will stay with her for at least twenty four hours?'

'No problem.'

Kate frowned. Was Daniel planning on staying himself? The last thing she wanted was to have him, or anybody else for that matter, hanging around in the morning, trying to stop her from going out in the van with the orders.

'How does the head feel?' her doctor asked.

'Not bad,' Kate said.

He raised his eyebrows.

'Well—to be honest—the lump hurts like mad and there seem to be little men inside my head banging away, desperate to get out,' she conceded. 'I think they're succeeding.'

'Right. A couple of paracetamol with a hot drink might help. Other than that, keep me informed of any changes,' he said to Daniel, closing his bag and picking it up. He nodded at Kate on his way out, and was gone.

Kate spent the next ten minutes trying to persuade Daniel to tell her why he just happened to be outside at the right moment, but ran into a brick wall. The more frustrated her attempts became, the more relieved Daniel appeared to be. She eventually had to admit defeat. He wouldn't be moved.

'Daniel?'

'Mmm?'

'Thank you again?'

'What for?' he asked, as he lounged on the

Victorian chair, looking totally at home.

'For everything you've done for me tonight. I'm very grateful.'

'You're welcome.'

To Kate's dismay, her tummy chose that moment to rumble.

'When did you eat last?' he asked.

Kate lowered her eyes, giving the matter some serious thought, screwing up her face in concentration. 'Lunchtime, I think.'

He gave an exasperated sigh. 'No wonder your tummy's rumbling. You must be starving.'

She nodded. 'I usually eat properly, but I've been too busy—I'm not completely stupid, you know.'

'I don't think we'll take a vote on that right now, all the same,' he commented, heading for the door. 'I suppose you do have something to eat in your kitchen?'

'Of course I do,' Kate retorted huffily, mentally going through the content of her fridge. 'Lots,' she said, vaguely.

'Good.'

A short time later Kate was propped up on pillows which had been pummelled to within an inch of their lives and Daniel was sitting on the bed spoon-feeding her from a bowl of gruyere and broccoli soup, the appetising smell of toasted wholemeal bread coming from a plate on the bedside table.

'Are you feeling any better now?' Daniel asked.

'Much,' Kate replied, between sips of soup. 'The pills are beginning to work, too.'

'Good. Then it's time to answer a few questions, I think,' he said, a hard edge creeping into his voice.

She looked at him apprehensively. 'Me? Questions? Whatever for?'

He picked up a piece of toast and held it out in front of her. She bit a piece off and chewed it absentmindedly.

'How about this for starters,' he continued, spooning in more soup. 'Why did you phone the hotel and leave a message cancelling our date with the excuse that you had remembered a previous engagement?'

Kate nearly choked on the soup. 'What? That's a lie.'

'I know it's a lie, now. You had to admit to the police you were staying in. Why couldn't you just say you didn't want to see me again, if that was how you felt, or didn't you think you would get caught out?'

Kate rubbed a hand across her eyes. This had been a long day and it did not seem to be getting any nearer the end. One of us is going mad, she though, and I don't think it's me.

'That's rich, coming from you,' she retaliated, her voice rising and her temper well and truly lost.

'Who was supposed to be taking me out for dinner and then conveniently decided to forget all about it, and go out with friends instead?'

Daniel spooned her more soup and looked at her in amazement. 'Not me, that's for sure.'

'Don't expect me to swallow that,' she snorted, 'I heard you tell the police that you had been out with friends tonight. What have you got to say to that?'

Daniel's face coloured slightly and he hastily averted his gaze.

'Hah! Guilty!' The knowledge fuelled her anger. 'The least you could have done was to phone and let me know.'

He ran a hand through his thick hair, the unruly lock at the front giving him a strangely vulnerable look.

Vulnerable, Kate thought waspishly. He's about as vulnerable as a barracuda.

He glanced back at her. 'I tried to telephone all afternoon and no, before you fly off the handle, not to cancel our date. But every time I tried the line was engaged.'

'I am trying to run a business,' Kate shouted indignantly, 'or had you forgotten?'

'Of course I hadn't forgotten,' his voice rising to match Kate's. 'And stop shouting at me!'

'I am not shouting,' Kate shouted, 'you are.'

'I am not,' Daniel yelled.

The bedroom door opened, startling them both, and Kate's mother walked in, followed by her father. Kate put her head in her hands.

'My, my, you have been industrious,' she said, her voice querulous. 'This place is getting busier than Paddington Station.'

'We did knock, *chérie*,' Kate's mother said, crossing to the bed and planting a kiss on her daughter's forehead, 'but we didn't think you could hear us over your—er, discussion.'

'Hello, Mum,' Kate said, weakly.

'I'd like to know what the meaning of all this is,' David Hamilton commanded. 'We get a call in the middle of the night to say you have had an attempted burglary, you've been injured, the police have been and also the doctor. We rush down expecting you to be seriously injured, and when we get here we find you and this person shouting at each other.'

Daniel shepherded a surprised David Hamilton outside with him and closed the door, much to Kate's chagrin. He seems to be having a good deal too many conversations behind closed doors, she felt.

Kate exhaled a long sigh while her mother took Daniel's place on the bed. 'Daniel very kindly telephoned to tell us what had happened,' she explained, removing her coat and laying it on the bottom of the bed. 'We got dressed and drove down immediately. I must say, though, I was surprised to find you two fighting like that.'

Kate gave her a guilty look. 'He just seems to bring out the worst in me,' she said, shrugging her shoulders in a good imitation of her mother. She began, quietly, to tell her mother everything that had happened that day.

85

'. . . and that's about it,' she said, coming to the end.

'That still doesn't explain why you were shouting when we arrived, or why you are sitting in bed wearing a very glamorous nightgown and being fed your soup.'

Kate blushed. One lace and silk strap decided to fall down Kate's arm at that moment, and she grabbed at it, wrenching it back over her shoulder. Her mother looked at her knowingly.

'And don't go getting any funny ideas. It's not what you think,' Kate burst out.

'Of course it isn't, my darling.' Francine laughed. 'It never is. Now, why don't you try and get some rest?'

Kate finally lay back on the pillows, closed her eyes and let exhaustion claim her.

CHAPTER SEVEN

The sun was streaming in through her bedroom window when Kate woke. She stretched lethargically and, yawning, snuggled down deeper in the bed. Her foot touched the hot-water bottle and, instantly alert, she recalled the terrible ordeal of the previous night.

Through her open window she heard late-morning noises floating up from the cobbled street below. The metal heels of shoes tapping on the cobbles as people walked, the shouted greetings and laughter. Underscoring this was the splash and gurgle of the water running along the gulleys at the pavement edges.

She knew from these sounds that it was late and, as she lay in bed, she heard her own shop door open and close underneath her. Sitting up quickly, Kate glanced at her alarm clock. It read eleven thirty.

But that's impossible, she thought, disorientated for a moment by the pain that shot through her head with the sudden movement.

Surely I remember setting it to go off at six. She drew the offending clock towards her and saw that the alarm mechanism had been pushed down. No wonder she had slept so long. She eased herself gently out of bed.

'And just where do you think you are going?' Francine Hamilton demanded from the doorway. 'Back you go, Kate, darling,' she said, helping her daughter back into bed.

'But, Mum, I feel much better now, and anyway, I can't stay up here indefinitely. I've got a lot to do in the shop.'

'Not today. Besides, everything is being take care of,' she said, smoothing the duvet over her daughter's legs.

'How?' Kate asked, worried about the lateness of the morning and the orders which should have gone out hours ago.

'Just like your father—you must have all the answers to your questions immediately. But now, no more questions,' her mother said, holding up a hand for silence, 'until after you eat. Do you want a late breakfast or an early lunch?'

'Honestly, this is—' Kate began.

'Breakfast or lunch?' her mother repeated.

Kate sighed. 'OK, anything for a quiet life. I'll have breakfast,' she said impatiently. 'But I must be quick. There are orders to be delivered before this afternoon, and they can't wait. I trust I'm to be allowed out for a shower?'

Her mother gave her an old-fashioned look. 'Yes, but don't be too long. Then I will tell you what has been happening while you eat.'

Needing no further encouragement Kate took herself off to the bathroom for her shower. Her head still ached when she moved it sharply but, providing she was careful and only moved it slowly, she could cope with the pain.

As she stood under the warm spray of the shower, lathering the soap, her mind ran over all the logical possibilities, but nothing seemed to tie up. Sally couldn't come in because of Sam, and neither her father nor Jeff knew anything about running a shop. So who, in heaven's name, was downstairs?

And what about the deliveries? Pulling a large, fluffy towel from the rail, Kate patted herself dry. She would have to do something about the wedding orders soon. It would be more than she could bear thinking about to let down the brides.

She cleaned her teeth, swapping the outrageous nightdress of last night for a more demure pair of pyjamas, and was propped up in bed again when her mother came in bearing a tray laden with goodies.

The smell of freshly-ground coffee and warm croissants made her realise she was hungry. She broke off a piece of croissant, spooned on cherry conserve and popped it into her mouth.

'Right,' she said, still chewing, 'give it to me straight from the top.'

Francine Hamilton laughed and looked, for all the world, like the cat who got the cream.

'They are having such fun downstairs! I couldn't wait for you to wake up so I could tell you,' she said, excitedly.

'Yes, but tell me what?' Kate said, exasperated almost beyond endurance. She knew, from experience, that there would be no point trying to rush her mother, or she would only get half the story. Francine tended to get excitable and skip from one detail to another like a butterfly.

'Well, when we heard that you were to stay in bed for twenty four hours Jeff phoned Sally early this morning to ask her how to switch off the burglar alarm, so we could at least open the shop for you,' Francine explained gaily.

Kate, sipping from a glass of freshly-squeezed orange juice, nearly choked. The thought of her family trying to run the shop, and on a Saturday, too, just didn't bear thinking about. The vision of her parents serving at the counter, let alone trying to deal with the myriad questions fired at them all day by customers was too much for her.

Almost frightened to ask the question, she said, 'So, what happened?'

'When Sally knew what had happened to you she wouldn't hear of staying at home, but there was the problem of Sam, who refused to leave her.'

'I can understand that,' Kate remarked, 'he had a bad shock yesterday.'

'So, anyway, she had this brainwave. She would come in, and bring Sam with her. Only there was the small matter of his bed.'

Kate groaned inwardly, and wondered whatever was coming next. 'Oh?'

She took a mouthful of coffee, wishing, in spite of the hour, that it was a large brandy.

'Well, Jeff solved that by going to fetch Sally, Sam, the small camp-bed and plenty of books and toys to keep him busy. He is now settled in the stockroom, in his little bed, and Jeff is keeping him amused between filling the shelves under Sally's supervision. It also means that she can look in on him when the shop is quiet.

'And your papa is at home looking after the stud and doing the milking for Jeff. They have done well, *non*?'

Francine described what was happening downstairs as fun. Kate thought it sounded more like a circus. She took another croissant from the basket on her tray and pulled it apart.

'It certainly looks like it. Any ideas what has happened about the orders?'

'Oh, yes, they are all gone,' she said, waving her arms around. 'Sally assures me everything is taken care of.'

Someone knocked lightly on the bedroom door, and they both turned towards it.

It was Daniel, carrying a large bunch of roses. He came into the room and smiled at Kate. 'Hi. How's the invalid this morning?'

'Umm . . . fine . . . thanks,' Kate managed, tongue-tied at his arrival, the sight of him making her pulse race faster. He walked over to the bed, placing the flowers in her hands. Kate buried her face in the yellow, cream and white petals and inhaled. No hot-house blooms, these, but roses with an exquisite scent. Her eyelashes glistened with unshed tears. 'They're beautiful, Daniel, thank you.'

Her mother left, pleading more organisation to take care of, and taking Kate's breakfast tray with her. Daniel sat on the bed. They looked at each other for what seemed like minutes before they spoke.

'Daniel, about last—'

'Look, I think—'

He gave an embarrassed laugh.

'This is getting to be a habit,' Daniel said. 'You go first.'

'No. You go first.'

'OK. I owe you some sort of explanation, Kate, especially after last night. There's not a lot I can tell you right now—'

They heard the outer door of the flat being opened and Sally's voice. 'Hello there. Anybody at home?'

Just when Daniel appeared to be going to tell her everything! Kate felt frustrated almost beyond endurance with this new interruption.

Daniel ran a hand through his hair impatiently and spoke quickly. 'As soon as you are fully recovered we'll talk, hopefully without interruptions. OK?'

She just had time to nod before Sally came in, balancing a tray with three mugs and a plate of biscuits on it. Daniel helped her find room for the tray on the bedside table.

'Trust you to have to go one better than me,' she exclaimed. 'As if we didn't have enough excitement with Sam, you have to go and provide your own. Can't you keep out of trouble for two minutes?'

Kate laughed. 'I didn't do too well, did I?'

Sally glanced shrewdly from one to the other, noticing Kate's bright eyes. 'Have I interrupted something?'

Blushing, Kate grabbed Daniel's flowers

which still lay on the bed, burying her head in the blooms.

'No,' Daniel said.

Sally turned to Daniel. 'I just had to come up to see the invalid for a few minutes and I've got some coffee here for you, too.'

'Thanks,' he replied, 'but I'd better have it downstairs.' He stood up and kissed the end of Kate's nose. 'Don't go doing anything rash,' he ordered, picking up a mug of coffee and a couple of biscuits. 'I'll catch up with you later.'

Kate watched him leave, a bewildered expression on her face. 'What does he mean, Sally, about having his coffee downstairs?'

'He obviously wants to get on with what he is doing downstairs. He's working in the shop, but surely you knew that?'

Kate shook her head slowly, hearing the words, but having trouble getting them to sink in. Daniel? Downstairs?

'Here. For goodness' sake, drink this, it should be cool enough by now,' Sally said, practical as ever, thrusting another cup of coffee into one of Kate's hands and a biscuit into the other.

Kate munched on the biscuit absent-mindedly, scattering crumbs on the duvet. Sally sat down and wrapped her hands round her coffee cup.

'It was all Daniel's idea,' she started. 'I had a call from Jeff first thing to say Daniel had been on the phone and wanted to know what was happening to the shop today.' She tucked her feet up under her and got comfy.

'Apparently he was prepared to help. Jeff called me, and that's where I came in. I wasn't about to sit at home when you needed all the help you could get.' Her face flushed prettily. 'You know me, I hate to miss out on anything.'

Kate smiled gratefully at her friend, knowing how worried Sally must have been about her son, yet still wanting to come and help. 'What then?'

'We all arrived at eight thirty, and Daniel went out straight away with the first load of deliveries—the weddings and some others.' She smiled. 'He's not one for sitting around waiting for things to get done, is he?'

'Why didn't he tell me himself?'

'Who can say? Perhaps he had other things on his mind,' Sally replied, her expression innocent in the extreme.

Kate threw the remains of her biscuit at her best friend. 'Beast.'

Sally laughed, and finished her coffee. 'I must be going back, before Jeff comes to tell me he's run out of shelves to fill!' She kissed Kate. 'Seriously, though, don't worry. We're doing OK.'

Kate sat quietly after Sally had gone, having plenty of time to think about the events of the night, and, more especially, about Daniel.

He was an enigma. Secretive and not to be trusted on the one hand—hadn't he refused to answer virtually every direct question she had asked him?—but thoughtful and caring on the other.

Taken together with the spontaneity and rapport which had been between them since they first met, she knew, in spite of everything, that she was beginning to fall in love with him . . .

CHAPTER EIGHT

The midday sun danced on the water of the Helford River as the small boat's prow cut through the tiny wavelets.

Kate and Daniel, manning the tiller, sat in the stern in companionable silence, basking in the sunshine, the only sounds the chug of the inboard engine, the slap of water against the prow of the little craft and the occasional scream of seagulls wheeling in the warm air currents.

She had been woken that Sunday morning by an early phone call from Daniel.

'Do you have any plans for today?'

'No. Why?' she queried, yawning and stretching her sleep-warmed body.

'Do you feel up to travelling?'

Kate contemplated his question. 'Yes, I think so,' she said in surprise.

She had slept soundly again the previous

night and felt almost normal despite the break-in at her wine shop and the subsequent bang on her head which she had received when the would-be thieves ran off.

'Good. I'll pick you up at ten thirty. Oh, and wear something casual. Soft-soled shoes, too. Trainers or something . . .'

He had arrived promptly, pulling Kate in to his arms and kissing her very thoroughly.

'Mmm . . . that's better,' he remarked, when he finally lifted his head. Kate, totally bemused, had to agree.

And now here they were, making their way up-river, searching for a suitable place for a picnic.

They passed a sheltered cove where people were sitting on the sand. A few hardy souls were taking advantage of the heat by cooling off in the water.

Daniel steered the boat in and out of peaceful little creeks until they came across a quay which was perfect for their needs. Trees at the edge of a small wood sheltered them from the light breeze, and short tufted grass ran to the edge of the quay.

Kate spread out the travelling rug on a flat area of grass while Daniel deftly tied a rope around the neck of a wine bottle and gently lowered it into the water to cool.

Kate was deputised to unpack the hamper.

'Have you see this, Daniel?' she asked, lifting the hamper lid and examining the contents.

'No. I just asked Chef to make me up a picnic lunch for two. Why? Is there anything wrong with it?' he asked, concern creasing his features.

'Well,' Kate said, starting to laugh, 'I think you ought to come and have a look.'

Daniel peered in. On one side he saw a snowy-white, folded, linen tablecloth with a hand-written menu on top, on the other side were two crystal glasses nestling in a pair of blush-pink napkins which had been starched to within an inch of their lives. The pièce-de-resistance was a small but delicately arranged bowl of tiny flowers, in shades of pink and white, protected by the surrounding well-packed containers.

Kate looked at him, hardly daring to breathe. 'Daniel, she said at last, 'it's exquisite!'

He looked up from the hamper with a mixture of sheepish embarrassment and childish amusement on his face.

'I told him I wanted to impress you, but I think he's taken me at my word and gone overboard!'

His expression was Kate's downfall. She fell on to the rug, laughing until the tears ran down her face. It wasn't long before Daniel joined her. Weak from laughing, he rolled over and kissed her.

'I'm not sure I'll ever be able to forgive

him,' he said.

'I think it's fabulous,' Kate said, 'but let's start on it soon, all this fresh air has made me ravenous.'

They attacked the hamper with enthusiasm. Chilled almond soup with a cream and flaked almond garnish came first, followed by salmon steaks in a light herb sauce and fluffy rice. While they ate Daniel told Kate about his past.

'Until my mother married Jack I never knew a settled home life. She was a ballerina, almost always on tour, often abroad. I was sent to boarding school when I was eight and even had to spend my holidays there when my father eventually divorced her.'

Kate, coming from a sheltered and loving family, was dismayed by Daniel's revelations.

'By the time Jack came into our lives I was almost fifteen and on the skids, mixing with the wrong people, and generally making a nuisance of myself. He stopped all that and forced me to take a good look at myself. It wasn't a pretty sight. Then he made me take some decisions about my future. I admired him for achieving what he wanted. He asked if I would like to go into the hotel trade and pointed me in the right direction, sent me on the necessary courses, made sure I met the right people—'

'You're very fond of him, aren't you? That's why you stood up for him to Pa at the birthday party,' Kate said, as they cleared away the plates.

'He's been more than a father to me, Kate. I know he would never do anything underhand in business, which is why I can't understand the animosity between him and your father.'

Kate shrugged her shoulders. 'I don't know, either. Pa won't even discuss him with me. I just don't know what to say.'

'In that case, don't say anything, let's try to forget it. Why don't you look in the hamper and see if there's a pudding?'

The tropical fruit salad was eaten in silence, each busy with their own thoughts. They finished off the last of the wine and while Daniel was pouring coffee from a silver vacuum jug, Kate found a small box of chocolates and truffles in the hamper, which Daniel said had been made in the hotel kitchens.

*　　　*　　　*

Later, basking in the mid-afternoon heat, Kate looked up at a single, fluffy cloud passing slowly in the clear sky and sighed.

'That's a big one,' Daniel remarked, leaning on his elbow and propping his head in his hand.

'You still haven't told me why you managed to arrive at the shop in the nick of time the other night. How about telling me now?'

He frowned and avoided her gaze. 'Why

spoil a perfect day? It all ended well, surely that's all that matters?'

Kate wasn't satisfied. It had seemed like a marvellous coincidence at the time, but she didn't believe in coincidences.

She pressed him. 'Please?'

He frowned at her. 'I've got some ideas, but nothing I can discuss yet. Trust me, Kate, and I'll tell you when I can.'

She tried again. 'Please?'

Daniel stood up and moved towards the quay's edge, his back to her, hands thrust into pockets. 'All I can tell you is this—what I said to the police about having been with friends was true. When I got your message I wanted to phone you back straight away. Adele, who took your message, is the daughter of a friend of my mother's. She's been staying with us for a while.'

'So I gathered. She did tell me that she was a special friend of yours,' Kate said flatly.

He turned around and looked at Kate thoughtfully. 'She persuaded me that as it was late you had probably already gone out. At the time I thought she had a point. She suggested that as my arrangements had fallen through, I might as well go with her to visit friends for the evening.'

'Hmm, I'll just bet she did,' Kate said, who was realising that the woman was obviously a master at twisting other people's words for her own benefit.

When it became obvious that Kate hadn't any intention of expanding on her comment, he continued.

'We were back at around eleven, but I found it impossible to settle, and went out again for a drive. The storm was raging and man hole covers were starting to lift off in the square with the volume of water. I thought about the ground level of your shop and decided to see if you were OK.'

He paused for a moment as if considering his next words before he continued.

'I drove along the service road and saw that your garage was open and your car gone, so I presumed that you were still out. When I passed at twelve and again at one and you were still out—'

'Hold on a minute,' Kate said, interrupting him. 'you mean that you came around every hour to see if I was home?'

Daniel raked a hand through his hair, a gesture Kate was beginning to recognise was agitated, but why? And why had he been checking on her? She shot him a puzzled look.

He came over to sit beside her again, facing her.

'If you must know, I wondered who could be keeping you out until all hours on a night like that—'

Kate tried to interrupt, but Daniel talked right over her—'and I was surprised to find that I didn't want to know the answer,' he finished.

She stared at him in wonder. He was jealous. Daniel was actually jealous. To think that while she was working in the shop and then sleeping, Daniel had been eaten up by the thought that she was out with someone else. She hugged the knowledge to her.

'What would you have done if you thought that I hadn't come back?' she asked.

He groaned sheepishly, and pulled her in to his arms. 'I would probably have been around again first thing in the morning, banging on your door and demanding an explanation.'

Kate wound her arms around his body and buried her head against his shoulder. She could feel the heat of him through the cotton shirt. Visions of him demanding an explanation, and watching the expression on his face when she told him what she had really been doing, made her laugh out loud.

'So when you came around at two, it was just another of your hourly check-ups?' she guessed.

'Except that I was late. Some of the roads around the centre of town were almost impassable, and I had to make a detour, otherwise I would have been there when the men were breaking in.' He sighed. 'I might even have been able to stop them.'

Kate shuddered at the thought. 'And possibly have been seriously hurt in the process.'

He drew back and stared deep into her eyes. 'Would you have minded?'

She nodded, almost unable to speak. 'Yes,' she said, putting all the feeling she had for him in to the single word.

'But, Daniel, you know something about the break-in, don't you?'

Immediately his face closed up. 'Don't push me, Kate, I've already said I'm not ready to talk about it yet.'

She was surprised at his change of attitude, and disappointed. Despite the way she felt about Daniel, she made up her mind that if he ever wanted to see her again he was going to have to tell her what he knew about the night of the break-in. He was obviously hiding something, and Kate had to know what it was.

CHAPTER NINE

The day had started full of promise. Kate had been pleased to find the early-morning mist being burned off by the sun as she drove north on the motorway towards Bristol.

The traffic was light and, although she had allowed herself plenty of time for the journey, she hoped it would stay that way until she reached the city centre and could park the car.

Excitement bubbled inside her as she drove. Kate loved her work, but never more so than when she was doing something out of the ordinary, as today. She glanced at the wine auction catalogue on the passenger seat and smiled.

One of the major auction houses was conducting the auction, and Kate had seen a few exceptional wines in the catalogue which she hoped to bid for on behalf of a very special client.

He had been one of Kate's first customers when she opened her shop and they had hit it off straight away. A well-known musician, he had a home in Cornwall and came down regularly for the peace and solitude he needed to compose his music. Over the years he had come to trust her judgement, so it had been only a matter of a phone call from Kate and a discussion of prices to ensure her place at the auction.

Today was important for her, as she hoped to convince him, by the prudent buying of these wines, that she was well able to supply not only his Cornish home, but also his London base, which would be a considerable feather in her business cap.

The traffic slowed as she approached the city centre, and she easily found a space in a multi-storey car park only a few minutes' walk from the auction house.

Checking her hair and make-up in the rear view mirror, she adjusted the scarlet scarf she had tied in a bow at her neck, the only colour in an otherwise severe outfit; glancing at her watch, she saw that she had another half hour before the auction started, and decided to stretch her legs.

Waiting to cross the road outside the car park, Kate noticed a black Jaguar coming along the road. She glanced at it idly at first, as it travelled towards her, becoming instantly alert as she recognised the driver. It was Daniel.

Kate's eyes were immediately drawn to the glamorous female passenger who sat by his side, smiling across at him. The car passed by, Kate unnoticed, as he turned to speak to his passenger.

Seeing him with another woman was like a slap in the face to Kate, especially as he had telephoned her only last night. He had come straight to the point after their initial greeting.

'Any chance of having the day off tomorrow, Kate? I'm going up-country and I thought you might like to come with me.'

She had been sorely tempted. Holding him at bay was harder than anything she had done before, especially as they were becoming closer. Since the picnic he had phoned her practically every evening, and her resolve to have nothing to do with him until he admitted what he knew about her break-in was wearing thin.

'I should love to, Daniel, but I'm already committed for the day.'

'You're not trying to put me off again, are you?' he said, his voice teasing.

She laughed. 'I promise I'm not, but the date has been in my calendar for months.'

'I'm sorry—it would have been lovely to spend the day in your company again.'

Kate was surprised to hear the disappointment in his voice. 'Anyway,' she said, changing the subject, 'how is the work on the manor progressing?'

'Very well. Too fast as far as the builders are concerned, I think. I've got nothing to distract me and keep me out of their hair while they work. Got any suggestions?'

Kate had smiled at the thought of the builders being harassed by Daniel.

So much for disappointment, she thought, as she watched the car move into the distance and felt a chill knot in her stomach. He obviously wasn't interested in who's company he had, just as long as he had some. She wondered who the glamorous passenger was.

*   *   *

So—I'm in love with a two-timing man who couldn't care less about me, she concluded, as she dragged her mind back to the present, her heart heavy, in time to hear her first lot number called.

'Damn,' Kate said, under her breath, as the first 'lot' of wine she had been bidding for went under the hammer to someone else. Luckily there were still three more lots that she was hoping to buy for her client, so she was still extremely hopeful.

She moved slightly on the Dralon-covered gilt chair to see if she could get a view of the man who had outbid her, but he was sitting next to a pillar and the angle of her chair made it impossible to see around it.

Writing the price that the wine had finally reached against the lot number in her catalogue, Kate sat back on her chair and smoothed down the skirt of her charcoal and white pin-striped suit. Checking her top price for the next parcel of wine, she listened intently as the bidding started.

But things weren't going her way. Depressed, she watched as, yet again, the man behind the pillar raised his catalogue and started to outbid her. Her brows drew together in puzzlement. She had been pretty confident when she had estimated the price these wines would fetch, and so far she would have been right, as the only person against her at the end of the bidding was the mysterious man behind the pillar.

The next lot was also Kate's, a dozen cases of claret, made by a prestigious wine-maker in a year of near-perfect weather conditions. There were very few cases of this vintage for sale on the open market now, and Kate was determined to have them for her client so she was still extremely hopeful.

She didn't enter the bidding until virtually everyone had dropped out, and discovered, to her horror, that her adversary was also bidding. She nodded each time the auctioneer looked in her direction, hoping that it would be for the last time, but her mysterious man kept raising his catalogue. Kate, angry beyond belief, kept going until the wine was hers.

'Now beat that,' she declared smugly, as she smiled with triumphant satisfaction at the pillar. She had gone only slightly over her client's price for this bid and was happy that she would have something for him at last. Her elation was short-lived. The man behind the pillar moved forward and cast an icy glare in her direction. It was Daniel.

His glacial expression turned to one of surprise, and then delight. He stood up and moved in her direction. Kate rapidly overcame her surprise, quickly gathered up her catalogue and handbag and, turning in the opposite direction, fled along the row of people, banging knees and apologising as she went.

'Kate, what a marvellous surprise.' She was grabbed by the arm and swung around as Daniel's longer strides allowed him to catch up with her outside the auction room. 'Why didn't you tell me you were coming here today?'

'It's just as well I didn't, isn't it?' she flung at him angrily, trying desperately to pull away from him. 'How could you do this to me,

Daniel? I trusted you.'

'Now, hold on a minute, just calm down and explain what you mean,' he said, deliberately lowering his voice in an attempt to quieten her.

Shocked to find that she had nearly revealed how she felt about him, Kate shuddered. 'I mean the wines, of course, you outbid me nearly every time. You don't need them,' she stormed, her temper getting the better of her, 'but I do. They were for an important client.'

'But, sweetheart, I only just saw you, how could I have known you wanted them?' he queried, logically. 'I bought them for Polventon. We need some extra-special wines as well as our normal selection for the guests, so I thought I would try here today in the hope it might save me a trip to London.' He smiled at her. 'Is that so bad?'

Kate, now anxious to get away as fast as possible before she broke down completely, shot him a frosty look, her lower lip trembling slightly. 'Let go of me.'

'But, Kate—'

'I must go and pay for the wine that I have managed to buy,' she interrupted.

He gave her a long hard look and reluctantly released her. Kate turned on her heel and quickly walked away to the office while her legs could still support her.

Paying for the wine and arranging delivery

took some time, as Kate first dropped her cheque-book then her pen and finally the entire contents of her handbag spilled over the floor in disarray. Her hands were shaking as she wrote the cheque, and she hoped the bank would recognise her signature when it was presented.

She stood inside the door of the office and took a few deep breaths before leaving, trying to steady her nerves. As she opened the door Daniel, who had been leaning against the wall waiting for her, grabbed her hand and dragged her towards the entrance door.

He marched her on to the pavement outside. 'Look, Kate, I know how upset you must be, but they are only cases of wine, when all's said and done. You don't have to take it so badly. We can sort this out, I'm sure.' His hand went into his hair at the gesture she had come to know so well, and her heart lurched. She gazed up into his face, watching as it dimpled in a smile.

'Come and have lunch with me,' she heard Daniel saying. 'Let's go and find a pub and talk this over, what do you say?'

He couldn't have shocked her more if he had thrown a bucket of water over her. She twisted out of his grasp, backing off. 'What? With you and your glamorous companion?'

He looked surprised. 'What are you talking about?'

'I saw you earlier—in the car.'

'Oh,' his face cleared. 'That was just Adele.'

Adele. Adele Forrester—the woman on the phone the night of the break-in who had been so rude to Kate. She saw red.

'And is this to be a cosy little threesome? You, me and Adele? You must think I'm mad?'

'But, Kate, she's not with me now.'

She put a hand up in front of her to ward him off, and continued backing away. 'I won't listen to any more of this,' she cried, her voice uneven with emotion, 'and what's more, I don't ever want to see you again. Just keep away from me, do you hear?'

Turning away, Kate ran as fast as she could, heedless of Daniel's calls and the stares of people in the street who watched her go, intent only on putting as much distance as she could between herself and the man who had broken her heart.

* * *

'Kate, my dear, I think you ought to try and eat a little more,' her worried father said, offering her the dish of roast potatoes.

'No thanks, Pa. I'm not very hungry today,' Kate sighed, pushing the remains of her meal to one side of the plate and laying down her knife and fork. She gave him a wan smile. It's probably my own cooking I can't stand.'

'Rubbish. You cook well. Not quite the

111

delicate touch of your mother, but nothing that a little practice won't put right,' he said, reaching over to pat her hand reassuringly.

She smiled. 'Talking of Mum,' she said, changing the subject, 'what do you think she and Aunt Nell are doing now?'

David Hamilton looked into the middle distance and thought for a while before answering. 'Knowing Nell, I expect they are resting up today before going to another show tonight and then continuing the shopping spree tomorrow.' He shook his head. 'How those two pack so much into a day I'll never know, but your mother does enjoy her visits to Nell, even if they are only for a few days.'

Kate rose to her feet and cleared away their plates. 'You go and get started on the papers, I'll bring in the coffee when I've made it.'

'Thanks.' He planted a kiss on Kate's cheek as he wandered off in the direction of the sitting room.

Kate spooned ground coffee into the filter machine and added cold water, pain flooding her mind as it always did these days when she was on her own. It was nearly three weeks since that awful day in Bristol and her heart had been filled with a terrible ache ever since.

She leaned on the kitchen table waiting for the coffee to filter through and stared out of the window across the field towards the river.

Would she ever be able to get Daniel out of her mind? She lay in bed at night and felt his arms around her, felt his lips on hers. She stored amusing incidents to tell him, before remembering there would be no more shared laughter, no more looks of understanding when they caught each other's eye, as if they knew each other's thoughts without speaking.

Kate had found it impossible to tell anyone what had happened between them, unable to stand the pity she was sure would be in their faces. Her parents kept their own counsel, but she knew they were worried about her and saddened that she felt she couldn't come to them any more with her problems.

She was no longer able to hide the fact that she wasn't eating properly, her clothes told their own story, and she had seen Sally throwing her worried looks when she thought Kate wasn't looking. The circles under her eyes got darker and darker.

Kate bit hard on her lower lip and went to lay a tray for the coffee. When it was filtered, she took it through to the sitting room where her father was already lost in the pages of a large Sunday newspaper. About to pour her father a cup, she heard the crunch of tyres on the drive, and moved across to look out of the window.

A black Jaguar came to a halt. Was it Daniel? Kate's heart somersaulted then dropped to earth again. A tall, grey-haired man got out of the car.

'Who is it, Kate?' her father asked.

113

'No idea.'

David Hamilton came to stand behind her at the window. 'Good God—it's Jack Trevelyan! What in heaven's name does he want?'

Kate watched the man come around the car towards the door. He might not be Daniel's natural father, but there was a certain similarity in their style, their walk, which made them appear related.

'How should I know, Pa. I'll go and let him in,' she said, turning to go out of the room.

'No! I'm not seeing him. Tell him I'm out.'

'Don't be silly,' Kate said, over her shoulder, as she went to let him in, 'he saw you at the window.'

She opened the door. 'Mr Trevelyan, I believe,' she said, holding out her hand. 'I'm Kate.'

'Jack, please.' Returning her smile he took her hand in a bear-like grip. 'I see your father is at home. Might I have a word?'

She showed him into the sitting-room where her father was looking out of the window, deliberately keeping his back to the door.

Kate sighed inwardly. There was just no 'give' in her father at all.

'Would you care for a cup of coffee?' she asked, 'I've just made some.'

'That would be lovely, Kate, thank you.'

The temperature in the sitting-room had dropped several degrees by the time she returned with another cup and, on pouring one for their guest, Kate left them to it.

A few minutes later, hearing a car pull away from the house, she made her way back to the sitting room, where she found her father pacing up and down.

'Well?'

'Well, what?' her father demanded.

'What happened? What did he come for? Surely he told you?' Kate's face was alive with curiosity.

'To discuss the land.'

'Oh, Pa, that's great!' she burst out, hardly able to contain her delight. 'And?'

'And nothing.' He scowled at her. 'He won't sell.'

Kate's face fell. 'But what about renting?'

'How should I know? He left.'

She groaned. 'What did you say to upset him?' she asked, sinking into the nearest chair, 'I could hear you shouting, out in the kitchen.'

'I don't really know. One minute we were talking, the next we were arguing.' He stopped pacing and came over to where she was sitting. 'Look, I can't settle. I'm going for a ride.'

Kate knew better than to offer to go with him. Her father always preferred to work his anger out on his own.

*   *   *

After he left, Kate tried to settle down with the

115

papers. She had just finished reading an interesting article about one of the gurus of the wine trade when she glanced out of the window.

Halfway up the drive a horse was grazing on the grassy bank. Kate was on her feet and running out of the house in a flash, recognising it as the one her father had taken out. The horse spotted her and shied away, a leg tangling in its reins. She immediately slowed down and spoke softly to it, edging closer all the time.

'That's a good boy. Steady now.' Holding out her hand as if offering the horse a tit-bit, she said, 'Come and tell me what a clever boy you are, coming home on your own.'

The horse tossed its head, but responded, walking towards her and nuzzling her hand while she grasped the reins and untangled them from its leg.

Trying desperately to keep calm, she led the horse up to the yard, removed its saddle and bridle and turned it into the paddock.

She knew her father was an experienced rider, so was hardly likely to have been thrown by the horse unless it was frightened. He must have had an accident.

She ran up the lane in the direction her father normally rode and asked at a few of the cottages in the village, but no-one had seen him.

She couldn't take a car to search for him as

the road ran out in the village and became a bridle path. She didn't want to risk looking for him on her own in case she found her father injured, and had to go for help. It would save time to take someone with her—but who?

Her mother was in London visiting Nell, and Jeff and Sally had taken Sam to Lands End for the day, so who else could she ask . . . ?

CHAPTER TEN

She ran back to the house, her hand only hesitating a fraction of a second before dialling Trevelyan Court Hotel.

She sagged against the wall, gasping for breath. Would Daniel even talk to her, considering she had refused even his phone calls since the day in Bristol?

No point worrying about that, she thought, when Pa could be lying somewhere, injured.

'Kate, what can I do for you?' the voice said.

He sounded distant, and she was afraid to go on, but knew she had to. 'Daniel—it's Pa. His horse came back—I can't find him.' She knew she was gabbling, but couldn't stop.

'I need help and there's no-one here,' she managed to force out, 'Please?'

'I'm on my way,' the thawing voice said, and he disconnected the call. Relief swept over

Kate as she gently laid the receiver back on its rest.

When Daniel drove into the yard ten minutes later, Kate had already saddled up two horses and was waiting for him.

'What about a First Aid kit, just in case?' he asked.

'I've tied one on to my saddle,' Kate replied.

'Good. Any idea of the direction he took?' Daniel said as he mounted his horse.

'Yes.' Kate filled in the details for him as they rode, grateful to be back in his company, despite the seriousness of the situation.

They rode through the village and along the bridlepath as fast as they were able and within half an hour they had found David Hamilton, lying on a pile of last year's fallen leaves. He was conscious, but only just, and complained of pains in his arm and chest.

Daniel took charge, making her father as comfortable as possible. He used his mobile phone to call the emergency service for an ambulance, moving a little way away from the older man as he did so, not wanting David Hamilton to hear him voice his concerns as to the extent of his injuries.

The stretcher had to be carried through woods for part of the way and the journey seemed interminable to Kate.

Within a short space of time her father was in hospital, having the best possible care and attention.

Daniel must have left her side at some point, to have contacted her mother in London and left a message on Jeff's answer-phone, but Kate hadn't been aware of it, only remembering how he had kept her company until Jeff arrived, and held her while she sobbed uncontrollably with relief when the doctor told her that her father had only suffered a mild heart attack, but they would be keeping him in for a few days' observation.

*　　　*　　　*

Striding into her father's hospital room on Wednesday morning, Kate stopped in amazement at the sight which greeted her. Her father was sitting up and looking better than she had seen him for weeks. On one side of the bed was her mother. On the other side was, of all people, Jack Trevelyan. They had been laughing, and appeared to be very happy in each other's company. Her parents were delighted to see her.

'Well,' she burst out, pulling up a chair and falling into it after greeting everyone. 'What have I been missing?'

They all started to speak at once. David Hamilton held up his hand for silence.

'As this is my story, I shall tell it,' he said.

Typical Pa, Kate thought, smiling at him indulgently.

'I asked Jack to come and see me and we

have settled our differences, I'm pleased to say.' The two men looked at each other and smiled. 'We had a misunderstanding when we were young, didn't we, Jack?'

'Yes. Like brothers we were,' Jack said, 'until my father built the garage.'

Kate, puzzled, asked, 'Garage? But what difference did that make?'

'Well,' her father said, taking a sip of water from a glass on the bedside locker, 'we had always wanted to do something with our lives, Jack and I. Jack wanted a hotel, even in those days, didn't you?'

'Yep. And you just wanted to make money,' Jack replied, 'if I remember rightly.' They laughed.

'Anyway, there was this bit of land which I wanted to buy to build a garage on,' her father continued, 'but before I could buy it, building started and it turned out to be a garage, owned by none other than Jack's father.'

'I didn't actually know anything about it,' Jack chipped in, apologetically, 'but David didn't believe me, especially when my father made me go and work in it. In those days you did what your parents told you.'

'We didn't speak after that,' her father said, picking at the bedclothes. 'My fault, entirely. I thought Jack had pinched my idea and told his father, who then built the garage for him.

'He did try to explain, but, as usual, I wouldn't listen. I'm beginning to realise I do

120

that quite often.' He looked embarrassed. 'It wasn't until Jack came to see me on Sunday that I realised I might have been wrong, all those years ago.'

What he said struck a cord with Kate. If her father could eventually be persuaded to talk, so could Daniel. She would give him a last chance to explain his actions. Intuitively, she knew that Daniel was an honest person but, like her father, she hadn't trusted her feelings.

Her father was beginning to look tired. Jack Trevelyan got to his feet. 'I'm going now, David. I don't want to tire you out, now we've got years to catch up on. I'll be over to see you when they let you out, then we can sort out the details for renting you that land you need.' The two men shook hands.

'I'll walk down with you, Jack,' Kate said, kissing her parents and following him out of the door. They walked along the corridor and down the stairs in silence for a few minutes.

'Coming over to the house on Sunday was Daniel's idea,' Jack said. 'He's been on at me to see if we could do something for your father. I certainly didn't mean to bring on the heart attack though, Kate,' he said, worry lines creasing his forehead.

She put a hand on his arm and turned him towards her. 'Don't think that you were in any way to blame. I'm sure Pa doesn't. It had been coming on for some time. His blood pressure hasn't been good for years, but he wouldn't listen to anyone.' Both realising what she had said, they smiled at each other.

'At least he will have to take his health seriously, now. Anyway—umm—how is Daniel?' she asked, trying to appear unconcerned.

Jack glanced at her, shrewdly. 'Working himself into the ground.' They walked out of the entrance towards the car park. 'Spends all his time chasing the builders and decorators.' He laughed. 'He's driving them mad. They'll probably be delighted to finish this job.'

'Oh? So the hotel will be open on time, then?'

'Before time, if this rate of progress continues,' he quipped. 'He's over at Polventon today, actually,' he added, craftily.

They reached Kate's car, and she unlocked it, turning to Jack. 'I'm so pleased things are better between you and Pa,' she said, 'and I'm glad we'll be seeing more of you.'

'So am I,' Jack said, bending to kiss her cheek, 'very glad.' He helped her into her car and shut the door. 'I'll see you soon, Kate.' And with an enigmatic, 'Good Luck,' he walked away.

She was still contemplating his comment when she turned into the road that led to her father's stud and, more importantly now, Polventon Manor. She was determined to find Daniel and force some answers out of him, and there was no time like the present.

She eventually found him down by the water's edge, 'Having an early lunch,' one of the builders had said.

'Keep him down there for a while, if you like,' another cheekily rejoined, and they all laughed.

Daniel was sitting on the grass, staring out across the water, absentmindedly throwing crumbs to a flock of small birds. His shoulders slumped dejectedly, and Kate's heart went out to him as she moved towards him across the grass.

A twig snapped under her foot and the birds flew up in a cloud. His head turned sharply in her direction and when he saw her he jumped to his feet, his lunch wrappings and the remains of the crumbs falling to the ground. Brushing off his hand and pushing them in his pockets, he waited for her to reach him.

'Hello, Kate,' he said, his face serious. 'Any news—from the hospital today?'

'Yes. I've just come from there, as a matter of fact. Pa's coming along nicely. He hopes to be out at the week-end.'

'That's good,' he answered, turning away to look out over the water again.

His attention distracted from her, she drank in the details of his face, the face she knew beyond a doubt she would always love.

'I had quite a surprise this morning. Your father was at the hospital.'

'Oh?' He lowered his head, a glimmer of a

smile on his face. Kate saw it and began to feel hopeful. She went to stand between Daniel and the water, facing him, looking up at him, demanding his attention.

'Daniel, I want to thank you for the help you've given our family over the land. Jack is going to rent Pa some of it, did you know?'

'Yes,' he said shrugging his shoulders, 'but I didn't do much.'

Kate reached out and gripped his arms. 'Don't play down what you did. Because of you, two old friends have been reunited. I think that's wonderful.' Tears prickled the backs of her eyes, and she rapidly blinked them away. Taking a deep breath she went on, 'But if you don't tell me about the break-in I won't ever speak to you again, and I don't think I could live with that.'

He gazed at her intently, and answered her by wrapping his arms around her in a vice-like grip, tilting her head up and lowering his mouth to hers in a kiss of such pent-up passion it knocked the wind from Kate. Her head reeling, he clung to his shoulders in an effort to stay on her feet.

'Don't you ever do that to me again,' he demanded. 'I've spent most of the last week trying to get you out of my head, convinced you didn't want to see me again, and the rest of it wondering if I could risk coming into the shop without getting a bottle thrown at my head,' he said, ruefully.

Kate laughed.

'I wouldn't laugh, if I were you, or I shall exact a terrible retribution. If you want the truth, I'd better tell you.' He sat down again, pulling her to sit next to him.

'That night when I saw the men driving away in the transit van I thought I knew them.'

'But you told the police—'

'I know what I told the police, and it was true. I didn't get the registration number, but I did notice a gash down the side of the van which looked familiar. It wasn't until the next day that I saw it again—at the hotel.'

'At the hotel? But I don't understand . . . '

Daniel sighed. 'I did—only too well. It belonged to a member of our kitchen staff. I talked to Chef, and made a few discreet enquiries before I phoned the sergeant.'

'But why didn't you tell me?'

He shrugged, and turned to look out over the water again. 'I couldn't say anything until the police had asked their questions and come to their own conclusions in case I was wrong. Besides, I was so embarrassed about the whole thing. Imagine if you had to tell me that a member of your staff and his accomplice had broken in to my hotel?'

Kate thought about it and had to agree. She nodded in sympathy.

'I was going to tell you that day at the wine auction, but you didn't give me much of a chance to say anything.'

It was Kate's turn to be embarrassed and a blush crept over her face, until she remembered why she had been so mad at Daniel.

'What about Adele?' she asked.

'Adele?' Daniel looked bemused. 'What about Adele?' He turned to Kate and gathered her in his arms.

'Oh, I don't know . . . you seem to be around with her a lot, and she did say that you were a special friend.'

'That's wishful thinking on her part, Kate. I didn't have anything to do with her unless I had no choice. My mother was a friend of her mother's, as I told you. When Adele's mother died, mine carried on the friendship and invited her to stay, now and again. Neither Jack nor I have got any time for her, quite frankly.'

The tension Kate had carried around with her for weeks started to ease out of her body at his words.

'When you said you couldn't make it that day I was disappointed,' Daniel continued, 'but knew it wouldn't be long before I saw you again. My mother, who knew where I was going, asked me to give Adele a lift home, as she lives in Bristol and it would save her having to take the train. Quite honestly I was glad to do it to get rid of her. I could see her handiwork in the mix-up with the phone call on the night of your break-in and, as far as

I was concerned, she had outstayed her welcome.'

While he had been talking, Daniel had absentmindedly been stroking the back of her neck and Kate's breath caught in her throat.

Suddenly aware of what he was doing, Daniel smiled wickedly.

'I've got a feeling the time for talking is over,' he breathed, his voice husky with emotion. Kate just nodded as she lifted her arms and threaded her hands in his hair, pulling his head down for her kiss.

There was silence down at the water's edge for a long while and when they finally separated Daniel brushed Kate's hair away from her forehead, his eyes dark with desire.

'I love you, Kate, very much.'

Kate smiled up at him, mouth trembling. 'And I love you, Daniel, darling. I think I must have loved you since you kidnapped me from Pa's birthday party, even though I thought you weren't interested in me at the time.'

'Oh, really? And I thought you were more interested in the food,' he teased, his eyes alight with laughter.

A soft blush coloured her skin. 'Daniel?'

'Mmm?'

'Talking of food,' she said, running a finger-tip around the outline of his mouth, 'I don't suppose you've got any lunch left?'

He shook his head, capturing her finger with his teeth and nibbling the end of it. 'Gave it all to the birds, why?'

'I'm starving,' she confessed. 'I don't think I've eaten a proper meal for ages and it's finally caught up with me. I can't think what's making me so hungry,' she exclaimed, widening her eyes and trying to look innocent.

Daniel laughed, a rich, warm sound, which seemed to come right from his feet. Glancing at his watch, he said, 'If we run, we can get a late lunch. I can't promise you goose on the menu, but I know a man who has at least a dozen marvellous puddings, all waiting to be sampled. What do you say?'

Kate's face lit up. She threw her arms around him, burying her face in the wool of his sweater. 'Daniel Ashcroft—that's the best offer I've had all year!'

'Then I think I can go one better,' he said.

Kate looked up at him, head tilted to one side, brow raised questioningly.

'Will you marry me, Kate?'

She smiled at him, her face full of the same love she saw reflected in his eyes. 'I thought you'd never ask.'

ST. Mary's.

ST. Mary's.